CHEROKEE OUTLET

CHEROKEE OUTLET

D. B. Newton

This Large Print book is published by BBC Audiobooks Ltd, Bath, England and by Thorndike Press®, Waterville, Maine, USA.

Published in 2005 in the U.K. by arrangement with Golden West Literary Agency.

Published in 2005 in the U.S. by arrangement with Golden West Literary Agency.

U.K. Hardcover ISBN 1–4056–3449–9 (Chivers Large Print)
U.K. Softcover ISBN 1–4056–3450–2 (Camden Large Print)
U.S. Softcover ISBN 0–7862–7893–5 (British Favorites)

The text of this Large Print edition is unabridged.
Other aspects of the book may vary from the original edition.

Set in 16 pt. New Times Roman.

Printed in Great Britain on acid-free paper.

British Library Cataloguing in Publication Data available

Library of Congress Cataloging-in-Publication Data

Bennett, Dwight, 1916–
Cherokee outlet / by Dwight Bennett.
p. cm.
"Thorndike Press large print British favorites."—T.p. verso.
ISBN 0–7862–7893–5 (lg. print : sc : alk. paper)
1. Large type books. I. Title.
PS3527.E9178C47 2005
813'.54—dc22 2005013459

CHAPTER ONE

Here was the land. Six million acres of it, by government survey—rolling red earth with wild plum and grape in the hollows, and bluestem that had been cured out by the smashing sun of mid-September. Over the years, plowshares had been busy ripping up the rough prairie sod of a virgin territory that stretched clear from Texas to the Dakotas. Now only this much was left.

This was the last of it. After it was gone—after tomorrow, at noon—there wouldn't be any more . . .

Such thoughts sat heavy on Lee Stormont as he rode his blue roan up out of a stream bed that was no more than a glistening streak of sand, in this tail-end of merciless summer drought. He pulled in, seeing a trio of riders in the empty middle distance; they saw him at the same moment, and quickly altered their course to come quartering in his direction. They were soldiers, blue-clad and stiffly erect in McClellan saddles. He held where he was, to wait.

The south wind at his back rattled through the paper-dry leaves of cottonwoods lining the draw. A scorching wind, without letup. Stormont lifted wide shoulders within the scalding dampness of his shirt. Watching the smear of sunlight flashing off polished buttons and cavalry insignia, he knew a fleeting sympathy for the men in those woolen army uniforms. He was sitting motionless, hands resting on the saddle swell, when they reined up in a rattle of bit-chains and accouterments.

'Warm day,' he said.

One of the troopers was a noncom, one a private. An officer led them—a second lieutenant, young of face and possessed of a stern dignity that had begun to wilt badly with the sweat streaming down reddened checks and into the collar of his tunic. This man said, without preliminary, 'You got business in the Strip?'

'Here's my permit.'

Stormont fished it out of a shirt pocket and handed it over. While the cavalry horses stamped and blew and shook sweat from their manes, the lieutenant read the paper carefully. He handed it back. 'So you work for Chapman?'

'That's right.'

'Well, I hope you realize all these passes are void at sundown.'

Stormont slanted a look at the brassy ball of fire frying the sky and the plain beneath. His skin was dark with a lighter pattern of creases about the eye corners, put there by years of such squinting into fierce prairie light. 'There's some time left,' he commented. 'I'm sort of taking a last look. I wanted to remember.

Twenty-four hours from now, a man will be hard put to believe it was ever this way.'

'Twenty-four hours from now,' the sergeant muttered, 'it won't be the Army's worry any longer! A fine chore we got, keepin' one jump ahead of a lot of land-crazy—'

'That will do, Sergeant!'

The noncom, a tough-skinned veteran, merely shrugged behind his officer's back and made a face. He leaned far out of saddle with his mouth working up to spit onto the burned ground; but his throat must have been cotton-dry, for nothing came out. He settled back, the gesture incompleted.

'Just remember,' the officer continued, his eyes on Stormont. 'You be out of here by sundown or you'll get the same treatment as any other trespasser. I suppose you've heard the name that's being used for people caught trying to sneak in before the deadline?'

' "Sooners." Yeah, I've heard.'

'Our authority goes no further than moving them out again. But, with a couple hundred thousand land rushers crowding us there's little enough we can do, if they should happen to lay hands on one of these men, themselves!'

'I don't need the warning, Lieutenant,' Stormont said bluntly. 'The last thing I'm interested in, is trying to grab off a homestead claim tomorrow—legal or otherwise!'

His curt tone of voice stung the officer, turned him even redder. The old sergeant spoke up. 'You talk and look like a cattleman. Would you be one of them that Benjamin Harrison had us move off the Strip, couple years back?'

Stormont nodded. 'As a matter of fact, I was.'

'Uh huh. Thought as much—and no wonder you feel bad about what them boomers are gonna do tomorrow! What iron'd you work for?'

'My own. Boxed S. It wasn't one of the big ones, but I was building me a herd.'

The sergeant shook his head. 'What a dirty deal that was, Lieutenant! It was the Cherokees' land—a permanent Outlet, the government said, for their huntin' parties to reach the buffalo grounds. But the damned farmers' lobby was slobberin' over it, and the Cherokee Council wouldn't sell long as they had the lease money the cowmen was payin' 'em.

'So President Harrison signed the order canceling the leases, and we had to move the herds off—with winter coming and no place to move 'em to. Rottenest piece of work I ever—'

'Sergeant!' The young lieutenant spoke in exasperation. 'I've warned you before! Keep up that kind of talk and I'll have to report you!'

'Yes sir.'

The lieutenant faced Stormont again. 'Remember what I told you,' he said crisply.

'Sundown. We can't make any exceptions.'

'I can look out for myself.' Stony of face, Stormont sat and watched the officer motion to his men and turn away. As they lifted into a lope, the sergeant looked back with a grin and friendly lift of the hand, which Stormont answered.

Watching them go he asked himself. Now, why'd I have to treat the boy like that? He was only doing a job . . .

This heat, that was it, he supposed. A hundred in the shade at least—had there been any shade, to break the lingering grip of an abnormal summer. He felt drained by tiredness, knowing he'd been at his job too long without letup.

But there was much more to his bitter mood. There was the thought of an era's passing, and of what tomorrow would bring to this Cherokee Outlet. Stormont had driven cattle across its hills when blue northers came whistling down from Kansas, and had shot his meat on the wing or running free and wild along the stream bottoms. He knew, better than many another, how the signal gun that fired at noon would end this last frontier and turn it into something beyond any recognition.

But he had taken his last look and there was no excuse to linger. The soldiers were out of sight by this time. Stormont had the reins and was shoving his boots deeper in stirrups, when a sound in the brush behind him made him twist about. A hand moved by instinct toward the sun-warmed metal of the gun in his holster.

Then he let it slowly fall away again, astonishment breaking through. He stared at the man who walked his horse out of the screen of cottonwoods, ducking a low branch and then straightening as he came into the open.

'Hi there, boy!' Bill Ivy's grin, and his greeting, were as casual as though three days and not three years had passed since they last met. 'Guess the coast is clear?'

'What in the world are you doing in here?'

'Waiting, mostly, for the Army to get done talkin' and leave.' Bill had reined in close and now, grinning, he reached to punch his old saddlemate on the shoulder with a fist. 'Why, damn!' he breathed, as the horses veered and settled. 'I knew it was you, minute I seen how you shaped up in the leather. For a minute I was afraid you'd get away before I could say hello—me not having any piece of paper to show the looie.'

'It's a risky business,' Stormont told him, frowning, 'to be in here without a pass.'

'Think so?' Bill Ivy snorted. 'Hell, the crick bottoms are swarming with sooners! Any fool could slip under the military's noses, with only half tryin'. Chief danger is the risk of cookin' and blowing away in this wind.' He sleeved a parched mouth, shook his head. 'Never seen it so dry, here!'

Stormont was searching his friend for signs of change, but three years had failed to tell on Bill Ivy. He would be near Stormont's own age—just thirty, in fact—but he looked younger. Strong sunlight had bleached out his yellow hair, until it showed almost white beneath the sweated hatbrim. There was audacity in his grin. His hazel eyes seemed to be all surface, giving a man back his own image but not revealing much of what lay behind.

'I'd have said you were a thousand miles away!' Lee Stormont told him.

'I was. New Mexico, Nevada, Oregon . . . I been punching cattle about everywhere from here to Christmas. But, I drifted back—wanted to see the big show tomorrow noon.' He gave the other's shirt pocket a significant look. 'And what the hell *you* been doing, to rate yourself a military pass?'

Stormont explained, briefly. 'Me and the man I work for—Tom Chapman—we've been hauling lumber and supplies to build the registry offices for the run. I've had to come and go.'

'A freighter, huh? When did you quit the cattle business?'

'I lost my taste for it, the time we all lost our shirts—when the government kicked us out of the Strip. Went to work for Chapman in Colorado. I've been with him three years.' He added, 'If you're looking for a mule-skinning job, I can fix you up.'

Bill Ivy shook his head. 'It don't appeal. I'm fixin' to get me a piece of land tomorrow.'

'You, Bill?' The other stared. 'Turning sodbuster?'

'Oh, hell no! This is to sell. For quick cash. I got a quarter section in mind—that bottom land at the fork of Pecan Crick. Remember?'

Stormont nodded. 'Good land.'

'Best pasture in the Strip. Ought to be some punkin roller willing to shell out for the relinquishment, and the chance to sink a plow in it.'

'What do you plan? To camp out here overnight?'

Bill shot him a keen look; then that brash grin broke once more across his face. 'You mean, sooner it? Aw, hell! More fun to play it their way, and show these rubes up at their own game. It'll be a wild thing, when the signal gun lets go tomorrow—I wouldn't miss it! I ride a sure-footed bronc, I know the piece of ground I want. I'm on my way right now to check the corner marker . . .'

Bill's glance turned eager with a new thought. 'What's the chances of ridin' with me? Grab the quarter just below mine—we can witness for each other; and two gents with guns might even hold onto their claims. What do you say?'

But Lee Stormont shook his head, and his

mouth settled into uncompromising lines. 'No, Bill. Not me—not ever! I loved this land; I'll not be the man to drive a stake in it! I've got my job to do for Chapman. But when that's finished, I never want to see the Outlet again!'

Such unexpected vehemence seemed to startle Bill Ivy, widening his eyes. 'Takin' it pretty hard, ain't you? Well, I know how you feel! It was a beautiful country—the last of the open range; and now it's gone. But this was bound to happen. What's anyone to do about it?'

'Nothing.' Stormont shrugged, and picked up the reins. 'I'm just letting off steam, Bill. Forget it. All the same, I'm not staking any quarter sections!'

'Have it your way!' But with the leathers in his hands, Bill Ivy hesitated. 'You gonna be anywhere around, this evening, where I can find you?'

'We've got our headquarters in Caldwell.' It was a Kansas town, a couple of miles above the line.

Bill nodded. 'I'll look you up—have a drink for old times' sake. If there's likker enough in that town to cut the thirst I'm gonna have by then!' He scrubbed parched lips on the back of a fist. 'Man, oh man!' Then his mouth widened, showing his teeth in that flashing grin. 'Well—be careful, boy!' His head jerked in farewell as the sorrel leaped under the stab of spurs.

And Stormont let him go, watching rider and mount dwindle across the sun-smeared distance.

Seeing Bill Ivy again, so unexpectedly, had awakened warm memories. Those had been great times, three years ago here in the Outlet. But they were past; Stormont shoved useless thoughts of them away, and speaking to his roan, rode on—filling his eyes for the last time with this land that, after tomorrow, would become a place past recognizing.

Red-soiled, streaked with watercourses, the Outlet lay wide and inviolate beneath the blazing sky. Far off, steel of a railroad flowed in molten, reflected light. A lone mule deer moved across the grass, stopping to nibble and then drift on.

Glancing down into the long grass at his roan's feet, he saw a government surveyor's corner marker—the four holes waiting to receive the claim stakes, and in the center the mound of raised earth and the stone slab. Lips moving silently, Stormont read the symbols that indicated range, township, and section. This, he thought ironically, was the future. Tomorrow, sweating men would scramble for the privilege of driving their stakes here and sinking their greedy plowshares. They needn't think, just because they owned a homestead patent, that they owned the land. Under that kind of treatment, the land itself would die. They would be left with nothing but a corpse . . .

*   *   *

There could hardly be any doubt when a man reached the northern boundary of the Strip. This side the invisible line was nothing; beyond it the clutter and noise began. Even with a blistering wind at his back, Lee Stormont could pick up the din from a mile away—the hum of sound that swelled as he neared, becoming a raucous punishment for ears accustomed to loneliness and silent places.

He jogged slowly nearer, dark face drawn into hard lines. Behind the shimmer of baking air, under a dust-haze mingled with the smokes of a thousand cook fires, the multicolored mass seemed impenetrable as a wall that stretched from east to west, beyond the limits of sight; but as he drew closer the pattern began to sift itself out. He could see the individual shapes of people, now, and horses, and every kind of conveyance—buckboards, light two-wheeled carts, surreys, canvas-sheeted prairie schooners . . . anything that had managed to roll to Kansas. Children swarmed underfoot; a pack of mongrel dogs went tearing through the swelter, setting men to cursing and frightening their horses.

A lone cavalryman patrolling the boundary saw the rider jog up out of the immensity of grass and started over as though to challenge him, then appeared to change his mind. Almost at once, as the noise and smell of the encampment engulfed him, Stormont found himself pocketed by a bunch of idlers who had watched him ride out of the Strip and now came crowding around with questions.

'Where you been to, mister?'

'What's it like?'

'Run across any sooners?'

There were city men with peeling, sunburned faces—gaunted farmers—men of every sort and background, alike only in their hunger for cheap land. Stormont was in no mood to bother with them. He gave them a glance and would have gone past without answering. But suddenly an angry voice shouted, 'I'll bet *he's* one of them damn' sooners! What the hell else would he been doing in there?'

He didn't wait for the thought to take hold. Without hesitation he slid his gun from holster and watched the group break and fall back before it. A man who had been reaching for the bridle jerked his hand away as though he had been burned.

'Stay back!' Stormont warned them. He would have used the gun if he had to, and they must have realized it. They held motionless, scowling and threatening. When he nudged the roan ahead, gun still leveled, they let him go.

He rode on, stony-faced, through litter that was like the remains of a million picnics. At one point he had to swing wide of a long queue of men and women lined up at a wagon tailgate, where a fat man with an umbrella for a sunshade was ladling tepid water from a barrel—at a dollar a drink. But at last the jostling mass thinned out into scattered camps, as he struck the section road stretching north the two miles to the town where he was headed; here, he was able to let the roan out a little.

Up the way there appeared to have been an accident. A prairie schooner, its canvas dirt-streaked from the miles it had traveled, had lost one of its big rear wheels and was slewed around half into the ditch; but the other landseekers pressed by in a steady stream without slacking or paying heed. It didn't look like much of an outfit, and Stormont thought sourly, Renters. A starved-looking team had been unhitched and let to graze; a woman, swollen in pregnancy, held a ragged little girl by the hand while she watched her man, and a boy of ten or so, work on the crippled wagon.

They had lifted a brass-bound trunk from the wagon bed and were using it as a fulcrum, with a spare wagon tongue for a lever. The boy lay on his stomach across the end of the pole—teeth clenched, face red, legs kicking wildly. But his weight wasn't enough to jack up the heavy, tilted box so his father could work the wheel onto the iron skein. Riding up, Stormont heard the man saying with tired patience, 'All right, son. Try again. Just a little higher.'

Here was a need that brought Stormont, however reluctantly, out of the saddle. He grabbed the pole's upward end and put the strength of his arms to drag it down; muscle corded tautly across his shoulders, and the length of hickory came level and he set his knee on it as the farmer cried, 'That's it! Hold her there!' The wheel slid into place, the clevis pin found its hole. The man gave the wheel a spin and then stepped back quickly. 'Now let her down.'

Stormont grunted, 'I got it!' The boy slid off the pole and he allowed the end to rise, carefully, until the wheel had settled and was free. Straightening with sweat trickling hotly down his ribs, he pulled the wagon tongue from underneath and dropped it into the dirt, beside the old trunk. He turned, to see the farmer wiping his face on a faded shirttail.

'Thanks, mister!' the man panted, eyes grateful. 'That was mighty kind!'

Lee Stormont shrugged. 'Didn't look like the boy was having much luck.' He dragged off his hat and sleeved his own forehead, nodded a greeting to the woman. 'Guess you'll be all right now?'

'Busted a linchpin,' the farmer said. 'Just lucky I had an extra. Pesky wheel!' He gave the thing a kick. 'Tire loosened when she dropped off. I'm sure as shootin' gonna have to do some work on it tonight!'

Stormont paused to give these people and their outfit a closer look. Everything about them spelled poverty. But lashed to the side of the wagon was the thing that made his mouth pull down hard. It was a grasshopper plow—a tool designed for turning the tough sod of unbroken prairie . . .

Something prompted him to say, 'You aren't going to try making the run in a wagon?'

The man shook his head quickly. 'Way we have it figured, Jody and me will take the horses and once we've got our claim staked, I'll stay on the land while he brings the team back for Martha and Sis and the outfit.'

He had a level, thoughtful way of talking that impressed Stormont. He didn't seem like the usual ragtag, greedy run of rent farmers; there was something solid and reassuring about him. His face held honesty and intelligence. He was, Stormont judged, thirty-five or so; his wife, like himself, had the fined-down look of a hard existence. As for the boy Jody, he was a miniature of his father. Towheaded, brown-eyed, barefooted, he reminded Stormont a little of himself half a life before.

Stormont asked the farmer, 'Where you come from?'

'Wisconsin. Yaeger's the name—Gib

Yaeger.' Stormont introduced himself and they shook hands; the farmer's grip was strong and horny, with blunt fingers scarred and broken-nailed.

'You've come a long way, to make this run!'

The other rubbed a palm across the back of his neck. 'Well, I'll tell you how it is,' he said, frowning at the smudge of dust and cookfire smoke lying across the sky to southward. 'All my life I've worked other men's land. Gettin' by all right—I can't complain—but still never far enough ahead that I could hope to buy a place of my own. Got nothin' in the world but this wagon and what's in it.' He shook his head. 'Rentin'—it's a hard life! Man should feel that the labor and sweat he puts in counts for something, instead of just improvin' the value of the land he works for somebody else. Sort of takes the spirit out of him, after a while.

'I wanted awful bad to make the run three years ago in 1890, when they opened Oklahoma Territory; but, I just wasn't fixed to do it. Been savin' and scrimpin', ever since. And this time, I'm ready!'

Stormont frowned. 'What if you don't get our quarter section?'

'I'll get it,' Yaeger answered with quiet conviction. 'My chance is good as anybody else's. That's as much as a man should ask for!'

Next moment, as though the narrowing pressure of time suddenly prodded him, he was turning with a shout to the boy. 'Bring up the team, Jody. Martha, you and Sis better climb in. We got to find us our place to camp!'

A busy activity seized these people. Stormont turned thoughtfully to his horse; by the time he mounted, Gib Yaeger already had the heavy trunk stowed inside the wagon and was slinging the hickory tongue underneath, while Jody hurried out of the tall, dry grass leading the horses. Yaeger paused in his work to lift a hand in farewell.

Stormont returned the salute, and the boy waved too. 'Good luck!' Stormont called back to them, across the stillness. And was surprised to find, riding on, that he really meant it.

CHAPTER TWO

The town of Caldwell, Kansas, had known a various history. There was a time when Texas drovers en route to Abilene and Ellsworth had made it their first layover after crossing the Indian Nations. Later, with the railroad, had come a brief, rocky period as a shipping point for long-horned cattle. But that was all past, and the little clutter of streets and sun-baked buildings had subsided into the drab half-life of a prairie farming center.

So Caldwell would never forget this summer of 1893, or the thousands that had poured in, unendingly, to swarm the streets and crowd the saloons and stores and wake the long-dead echoes with a boisterous new voice. Their tents and wagon camps, spreading in all directions, threatened to swallow the town's few solid buildings. Meanwhile, on vacant lots and at the edge of the prairie, there had sprung up the monstrous canvas tops of temporary establishments, to help handle the swollen trade.

Where a clapboard station stood beside the railroad, Tom Chapman had set up a wagon yard. On a siding, sun-browned men were unloading a pair of boxcars directly into the high-sided freighters. Piles of boxes and crates stood helter-skelter, waiting to be moved. Pete Quilter, checking stuff out of one of the cars, leaped down to the right-of-way cinders as he saw Stormont approaching from the stock pens where he'd left his horse.

'Some more of these manifests for you to look over,' he grunted, waving a handful of sweat-crumpled papers. Stripped to the waist, Pete showed a torso heavy with rippling muscle. He could lift a hundred pounds straight off the ground, but paper work was beyond him. The stain of an indelible pencil marked his hands and circled his mouth. 'Gonna be spittin' purple for a month!'

Stormont thumbed through the bills of lading, folded and stuffed them in a pocket. 'Tom back yet?'

'Ain't expecting him. If he gets dickering with them farmers, he might jaw all evening.'

'Oh, I doubt that.' Stormont shook his head. 'Not today. I suppose you've got wagons ready to go out and pick up the produce he arranges for?'

'Whenever we get the word. And that reminds me. Station agent has a telegram. I told him to hold it for either Tom or you, whichever showed up first.'

Lee Stormont nodded, and headed for the clapboard shack, hot cinders crunching under his boots. The stationman had the sheet of yellow paper ready as he came up the platform steps. 'From Kansas City,' he said. 'Collect. It was delayed—the lines are clogged as hell.'

'What about the seven o'clock, westbound?' Stormont asked, fishing up some change.

'Should be on time.'

'That's good. Tom's getting in a half-dozen carloads of stuff.'

'Isn't all he's getting,' the man said cryptically, and at Stormont's look indicated the telegram in his hand. Standing there, Stormont unfolded it and read the brief message, with mixed feelings:

ARRIVE THIS EVENING STOP PROMISE I WON'T GET IN THE WAY
LUCY

That was all; and though the news wasn't unexpected it had him frowning as he turned away. Thought of seeing Lucy Chapman again filled him with a pleasant tingle of anticipation. Still, this was a very awkward moment for her coming. As he walked back into town, he found himself viewing the town with different eyes—wondering what impression its rawness must make on a young girl who had never seen the West, and who came to it from a sheltered background, with her mother and her aunt only recently dead.

Arriving at the hotel, an ugly, clapboarded sprawl of a building, he shouldered through a press of loud-talking men to the lobby desk and asked for Tom. But the clerk hadn't seen him—evidently he wasn't back from his day's trip into the farming country around Caldwell, and with train time hardly an hour away it seemed doubtful he would return in time to meet his daughter. Plainly, it was up to Stormont.

He got the key and climbed squealing, dusty stairs to his room, It was an airless, comfortless place, its thin walls dingily papered in yellow, with a musty carpet that was worn through beside the bed and in the corner by the washstand. There was a mirror, that was like looking at oneself through water; a chest of drawers with its knobs missing, a rocker and one straight chair, a curtained closet. Through the partition, sounds of a neighbor stirring about in an adjoining room were perfectly audible.

Stormont pushed aside the curtain and took a few articles of clothing down from their hooks. Kicked back on the floor of the closet, out of the way, was the slicker he had never so much as unrolled in the two months he'd been here. A drawer of the dresser held a clean shirt, some underwear and socks. He dumped all these on the bed; he would have them delivered to the wagon yard and find himself a place there to sleep—there wasn't the slightest hope of getting another room for Lucy Chapman, in this town and on this night.

Shaving, he gave his reflection a narrow, critical regard in the wavering glass. It was a strong face, he supposed you could say, if you were to waste thought in classifying it. Ordinarily a man who gave almost no thought to his appearance, he saw now that the coarse brown brush of hair no comb could tame had grown perceptibly shaggy. He tallied the weeks since he had bothered to have it cut and thought, with disapproval, You damned roughneck! He smoothed it back over his ears as best he could, and turned to put on the extra shirt which, at least, was clean.

Reaching for gun and belt, out of long habit, he stopped himself. With a shake of his head he decided to leave them where they were, hanging on the bedpost. He felt naked without them; but men didn't wear guns openly in the

Missouri town where Lucy Chapman came from, and he didn't want to greet her so.

He found envelope and paper, wrote Tom a short note and sealed it in together with the telegram. Downstairs he turned it over to the clerk, along with his key, saying, 'Be sure he gets this.' Then he went out on the street.

With three quarters of an hour yet before train time, Stormont walked into a crowded restaurant and found a place at the counter. As he ate he listened to the boomer talk. Two men were arguing over the way to tackle tomorrow's run. 'Who gives a God damn how fast that race horse of yours can travel?' one of them demanded. 'He don't know open prairie. He'll bust both your fool necks, the first jump!'

The man on the stool next to Stormont shoved a dog-eared book toward him, forefinger spearing a crude drawing of a government survey marker. 'You understand any of this?' the man asked complainingly. 'It cost me a whole dollar. Supposed to tell how to read them there cornerstones . . .'

'Give you something to keep you busy this evening,' Stormont suggested curtly, and got up leaving his greasy meal half eaten. As he headed for the door, he caught a glimpse of a cheap alarm clock behind the counter. Twenty minutes to seven.

It was a long time for an impatient man, not much accustomed to waiting with idle hands.

Someone hailed him; he turned and it was

Bill Ivy. Breasting the clogging tide of traffic, Bill put his dusty, stockinged sorrel to a hitch rack and swung down to tie. He ducked under the pole, shoving back his Stetson as he stepped up beside Stormont. 'What a mob!' he grunted. 'Ain't the sun makes Kansas hot, it's all these people packed into it!'

'Your business taken care of?' Stormont asked him.

'You bet. Spotted the monument, got the numbers memorized. It's a beautiful piece of land, all right—looks just the way she did three years ago. The pick of the lot.' Grinning, he laid a hand on his friend's shoulder. 'Come on, I'm spittin' dust! I'll buy you that drink.'

Stormont hesitated. 'Why not?'

On what had been a vacant lot stood the largest and busiest of the tent establishments. No signboard was needed to identify it; the sour whiskey reek pouring out its open front sufficed. Lee Stormont and Bill Ivy pushed through and took a place at one of the long plank counters that ran the length of the saloon tent, on either side.

The side walls had been rolled up, yet the heat and stench and uproar of sweaty men packed in here was all but unbearable. An overworked barman passed them their drinks and raked in the silver Bill Ivy tossed upon the dripping wood. Palming his glass, Stormont looked around.

'This,' observed Bill Ivy, eying the busy

gambling tables that filled the middle of the tent, 'is the kind of mint a man needs to have workin' for him! Who operates it, anyway?'

'An old friend of ours,' Stormont answered cryptically.

Bill lifted his shot glass, gave it a critical look and then drained it off, with a toss of the head. He gasped, and shuddered, and slapped the glass down hard.

'Rotgut!' he exclaimed. 'Last place I tasted anything as bad as this was in a booze runner's camp down in the Cherokee Nation. Remember? That time we—' He caught Stormont's expression, and his eyes widened. 'You don't mean'—he indicated the big saloon tent with the wave of a hand—'*this?*'

'Behind you,' Stormont said. 'He's looking at you right now.'

Bill Ivy came slowly about. The man who stood a little distance away was a bit under average height—stocky, with more than the start of a paunch. Sideburns ran long down the sides of full, ruddy cheeks. His face shone greasily with sweat, and there were great dark circles of it beneath the armpits of his white shirt. He wore his thinning hair combed carefully in a saddle, across a beginning bald spot.

It was the eyes a person was apt to notice. They were a pale ice-blue.

'Hello, Ivy,' he said coldly.

'Murray Lenson . . .' Bill picked up the half-empty bottle, waggled it to slosh the liquor around inside. 'Feeding your Injun whiskey to white men now?' A wicked grin pulled at his lips. 'Knowing what this costs you, you really must be raking it in!'

Color had stung Lenson's soft cheeks. Anger glinted in his eyes as he saw the attention Bill Ivy's loud voice was beginning to draw. He opened his mouth to speak, then shut it again and, instead, gave a jerk of his head toward the open front of the tent. And having done so he turned and moved in that direction, himself.

The two friends exchanged a look. 'He expecting us to follow him?' Bill Ivy wanted to know.

'Your talk got under his skin,' Stormont said. 'I can imagine he'd be a little touchy about that business in the Nations. He wouldn't like it made public.'

The other shrugged. 'Might as well find out what he wants.' He gave his belt a hitch and started after Murray Lenson, through the milling crowd, still carrying the whiskey. Stormont hesitated a moment, then curiosity prompted him to drain off his glass and follow.

By now sunset had touched the flat edge of the western horizon, and already a haze of dusk was beginning to settle. Shadows claimed the rutted street. A light or two burned in houses of the town, and a man with a ladder was preparing to climb and hang a lantern high on the central pole of the entrance of the saloon tent. Yet, late as it was, the street dust stirred continually under creaking wagon wheels and thudding hoofs. The noise seemed to mount as night drew closer.

Stormont found Bill and the saloon owner standing to one side, out of the crush of foot traffic. Bill leaned a hip nonchalantly against one of the taut guy ropes; Lenson, facing him, had both hands shoved inside his waistband, an angry scowl on his face. He was saying hoarsely, 'You talk too loud! What were you trying to do in there, make trouble for me?'

Bill Ivy sloshed the whiskey bottle. His answer was touched with amused scorn. 'Just why would I bother?'

He was making a mistake. Lee Stormont could see that, even if Bill could not. 'Things have changed,' he cut in. 'Murray Lenson isn't the whiskey smuggler he was when you knew him. He's an important man in Caldwell. You should treat him with respect!'

Lenson let his burning look rest on Stormont's dark face, sensing the sarcasm. 'Why, thanks, Stormont!' he grunted. 'Helps my ego, to hear you say that.'

'Why not admit a thing if it's true? Nowadays,' he told his friend, 'Lenson could buy and sell you or me, a couple times over. Naturally he doesn't like being reminded how he got his start.'

Bill Ivy looked from one man to the other,

his grin broadening as he caught a hostile undercurrent here. Suddenly he began to chuckle. 'Funny as hell, ain't it—to stand like this and remember that day down in the Nations! Don't recall how many barrels we dumped,' he went on, the hard stab of Lenson's stare turned and blunted against a cool indifference. 'But I ain't forgetting the shape of your face after Stormont finished working it over!'

'The Cherokees were good friends of mine,' Stormont said shortly. 'I couldn't stand by and watch somebody sell them poison.'

'Is selling it to a tent full of boomers any better?'

He shrugged. 'I figure this scum can look out for themselves!'

Lenson let his eyes go narrow. 'Interesting point of view, Stormont. Sounds almost as if you think more of a stinkin' savage than you do a white man! Maybe you think the Strip oughtn't to been taken away from them?'

'If I do or I don't, could hardly be important!'

'Oh, it might, it might. It could be important to your boss.'

Stormont shot him a look, trying to read his meaning. 'How?'

'Why, Tom Chapman hopes to build himself something solid, down there—Freight King of the Strip! Whether he does, depends on the good will of these same homesteaders you seem to think so little of.'

'I don't intend doing anything to risk it!'

'Let's hope not.'

At that moment a train whistle floated long and far across the Kansas prairie. Lenson fished up a silver watch from a pocket of his waistcoat, glanced at it. 'Seven o'clock's almost on time, again,' he remarked.

Jarred into remembrance, Stormont said, 'You'll have to excuse me. I got business.'

Before he could turn, Lenson interrupted him. 'One second—since you mention business. They tell me Chapman is thinking of that Comanche townsite, for his headquarters.'

Something turned Stormont cautious. 'What about it?'

'Why, I've had my eye on the place myself. It's a good location—will probably become one of the big commercial centers. So he and I may be ending up as neighbors.'

Lee Stormont thought, Now, why tell me that?

He looked at the other a moment, trying in vain to probe behind the opaque curtain of those expressionless blue eyes. There was dislike and even hatred there, he felt certain—a resentment tamped down but feeding, through the years, on the memory of a day when their paths had crossed, in violence, in the secret fastnesses of the Cherokee Nation. For the first time he heard a warning bell and recognized in Murray Lenson a potential for danger.

He said, coolly, 'That's something to look forward to!' Looking at Bill he nodded. 'Be seeing you. Thanks for the drink—such as it was!' And he turned on his heel and left them, his stride already lengthening as sight and sound of the train pulling in toward town put other thoughts from his mind.

The seven o'clock was a mixed train, day coaches and a mail car, and the rest in special freight. By the time Stormont reached the clapboard station it had pulled to a halt and the big engine was letting off steam. Noise, and the smell of hot oil and metal, engulfed the station platform. Passengers were getting off the train, while Pete Quilter with a crew of men waited for the freight to be released so they could unload. Stormont told them, 'I'll be with you when I can. Another matter I have to see to.'

He stood, oddly excited, watching the travelers pile out of the coaches and eager for the first glimpse of her. The rush ebbed, and with it the shouting of voices and the stampede of boots upon the splintered platform. For a moment Stormont thought something must have happened and she'd missed the train . . . and then he saw her, coming down the iron steps of the second coach.

She clung to the rail with one gloved hand, clutched a heavy carpetbag in the other as she timidly peered about her. She looked small, and young, and frightened. She was dressed rather severely, in an ankle-length traveling skirt and blouse, with a cameo pin at her throat—she must have had an uncomfortable time of it, Stormont thought, alone in a crammed and sweltering chair car. She stepped down, now, onto the platform; and Stormont walked toward her.

Dark hair curled at the edge of a smart little hat as she turned, quickly. Despite the heat she was pale. Her lips parted a little. Brown eyes stared up at him and then warmed with relief and pleasure; she managed the beginning of a smile. 'Lee Stormont!' she exclaimed. 'It is, isn't it?'

'That's right.' He was pleased she remembered. He'd thought often enough about that other meeting: himself sitting uneasy on the edge of an overstuffed sofa, in the parlor of that big house in a Missouri town; and Lucy Chapman smiling and chatting like a little girl, company-polite and secure in the familiar surroundings of her aunt's home. Tasseled table runners, potted plants, and gilded picture frames—such had been Lucy Chapman's world. To Lee Stormont it was a world unfamiliar and even suffocating; but Tom Chapman had asked as a special favor, that time he went back on business, if he'd stop and look in on his daughter. It was a request he couldn't have refused, filled as it was with pathetic longing for some word of the child Tom hadn't seen in over a dozen years . . .

His hat awkward in his hand, Lee Stormont managed now the words he supposed he ought to speak. 'I was sorry to hear about your aunt.'

Recent pain touched her face and made her look suddenly tired, with more than the weariness of the journey. 'She was quite old,' Lucy Chapman said. 'But it was a long, hard illness.' Hard for the girl, Stormont thought. So young as that, and to have had these losses so quickly following each other—first her frail mother, and then the aunt whose death had meant the final breakup of her way of life.

Now he was the one who stood solidly on native ground, where he belonged; he was filled with sympathy as he watched her peering off toward the empty prairie, darkening now with twilight. The thought struck him: Why, I'm the only familiar thing to her, here! There'd be her father, of course—but she wouldn't remember Tom Chapman. It had been so many years; she was only a baby when her mother, too weak to stand against this frontier, had broken and fled from the land and the man who was a part of it.

Stormont said quickly, 'I'll take your bag. We've managed a hotel room for you. Things are pretty much upset—after all, the run is tomorrow, at noon. But, we'll make you comfortable.'

'Thank you,' she said, with real gratitude. 'I

know I'm going to be a nuisance!' She pushed a strand of loosened hair back under her hatrim, and sighed. 'But if I could only have a bath! I've never been so filthy . . .'

'I bet that can be arranged.'

He saw now she was staring in awe at the noisy stock pens, at the big freight wagons whose canvas covers gleamed in flickering torchlight. 'Your father's,' he explained, hoping it would interest her.

'*All* of them?'

'Every one! And loaded with freight—ready to roll across the line the minute the dust settles. Do you realize, tomorrow this time there'll be a whole new Territory, with thousands of settlers—and except for one railroad line, every stick of lumber and scrap of food and supplies for them will have to follow them in over the wagon trails! And Tom Chapman means to have the bulk of that business.'

Her lips rounded in a silent 'Oh!' She glanced at him shyly. 'It—it's exciting, isn't it? And you're going to be in it with him?'

Stormont shook his head. 'Only while he's getting things started; then I'll likely move on. I'm a restless kind of man, I guess. Not used to so many people around me.'

A little frown tugged at her brow. 'Strange! That's *ex*actly what I've heard my mother say about—Pa.' The name came out a little awkwardly; probably she had lately been schooling herself to use it. 'She always told me he was restless!'

'Most of us are, out here . . .'

Stormont didn't say so, but he could imagine some of the things Lucy must have had dinned into her, through the years, by that weak and embittered woman who had lacked the fiber to be a mate to big Toni Chapman. Tom had never once blamed his wife for leaving him. He seldom spoke of her at all, but when he did it was in a softened tone and always with respect. He had sent money regularly, without complaint, even when the tide of fortune was against him and he could ill afford it.

For he had deeply loved his wife—the gentility which had awed him, and which he couldn't hope to match. Life without her and their child had been cruelly empty, yet Tom had been wise enough to realize they were mismated from the start, and that there was no more place for him in that other world, than for her in his . . .

'Tom's got big plans,' Stormont said as the two of them walked along the crowded sidewalk. 'For you too, Lucy. You'll be the belle of Comanche! Have the biggest house in town, wear the prettiest clothes, drive a buggy behind a fine team.'

He was grinning as he told her this, and the girl made a face at him and then even laughed a little. Their talk had eased her nervousness, brought them closer; now he tucked his hand beneath her arm and she let it rest there. She really was a small thing, barely clearing his shoulder. Thin, too, but that would be from the strain of her aunt's long illness.

Full dark had fallen, but many lights came from open doors and windows, leaked through the canvas walls of tents, flickered with the night wind whipping the flares attached to building fronts. 'Hotel's right up ahead,' Stormont said, and the girl nodded.

Just then there was a quick swelling of sound behind them, a sudden yelling of men and scrambling rush of horses. Lee Stormont was turning to see what was bearing toward them when the first shots broke. Moving almost by instinct, he crowded the girl back against a building while his right hand, dropping her arm, went toward his hip. His fingers scraped jeans cloth before he remembered he'd laid his belt and gun aside. So, scowling, he stood with Lucy pressed against him, while a storm of confusion and hullabaloo blew up along the dusty street.

The earth shook to the pounding of hoofs, and the night seemed all at once filled with horsemen, with the shine of bridles and spurs, of lathered flanks and rolling eyeballs. He had a brief glimpse of a single rider in the lead—a desperate face, a hatless figure that crouched in the saddle and raked with the spurs. At that instant, the rider was overtaken and swamped.

A hand reached and dragged him from his horse, into the dirt. Quickly, saddles emptied as his enemies piled on him. More men came pouring out of Lenson's saloon tent, out of other places along the street. The yelling became a roar. After that one glimpse, Stormont couldn't find the one whose capture had started it all; he was lost somewhere in the mill of men and animals.

Lucy, behind him, cried in a choked voice: 'What—what is it?'

A riderless horse, maddened by the hubbub, came bucking out of the crowd. Its shod heels clipped splinters from the wooden sidewalk; a muscled haunch swung about, narrowly missing them both. Stormont cursed and swung with the carpetbag. As it struck, the horse squealed in fright and jumped away; Stormont whirled and seized Lucy's arm.

'Let's get out of this!'

Someone running toward the scene of confusion slammed into them and Stormont shoved him aside with the thrust of an elbow that drove whiskey breath out of him in a gust. Then they were working through the crowd, Stormont, grim of face, making a way for them, Lucy trying to keep up. Behind them the mob noise had risen to a frenzy of hoarse screaming.

Free of the worst crush, Stormont slowed to look back, still keeping his firm hold on Lucy's arm. There was a knot of movement at the center of the crowd, that surged wildly. Once, for just a moment, the screen of men thinned and gave them a glimpse of a ruined, bloody face, and a body whose clothes had been nearly torn from it. Then this horror was engulfed, as Stormont moved to put himself between it and the girl.

Still, she had seen. 'What are they doing? Who—who is it?'

'Some sooner, caught trying to hide out in the Strip. He thought he'd shake them, once he reached town, but they were too close. Come on!' he added roughly; but she seemed incapable of moving. As though rooted, she stood and stared up at him in horror.

'But—they're *killing* him!'

'Maybe. Nothing anyone can do. Too many of them—too worked up. Shut your mind and try to forget it!'

She shook her head, blindly. Her mouth trembled and her eyes, in the poor light, were dark holes in the pallor of her face. '*Forget!* How can you say such a thing? How could anyone—?'

Not trying to answer, Stormont turned her and made her walk with him, toward the big hotel a block distant. The sounds behind them began to blend into the general tide of racket pouring and billowing along the thronged thoroughfare. A man laid a hand on Stormont's elbow, saying, 'Hey, friend! Something going on down there?' Stormont flicked him the briefest look, pulled his arm free.

The disturbance had not even reached as far as the hotel, and the men who moved across its veranda and through the lobby's open doors seemed totally oblivious of the thing happening a mere block away. As Stormont and the girl stepped off the sidewalk, to wade across through deep dust, Lucy stumbled and would have fallen except for the firm grip on her arm. She was physically exhausted and her nerves, he judged, must be strung to the breaking point.

Then they had mounted the three low plank steps and were entering the crowded lobby. And at once, Stormont saw big Tom Chapman, standing at the desk.

Dusty and saddle-tired, Tom had the envelope Stormont had left and was even then reading the telegram, with a stunned expression. Stormont moved forward, leading the girl. 'Tom . . .'

The big head turned, lamplight sheened on its thick mane of silver. Blue eyes looked at him questioningly, and then saw the girl at his side.

The man's fingers opened. The yellow paper fluttered to the carpet as Tom Chapman came around slowly, staring; his strong, handsome face, beneath its powdering of dust, was suddenly ashen.

'It's really you!' Chapman's hands lifted,

trembling with a long hunger; then, instead, he let them fall without touching the girl. He was, after all, a stranger. He couldn't force himself on her. These thoughts were plain in his mobile, expressive face.

'Lucy!' He spoke her name, and shook his head a little, all the stir and bustle around them forgotten. 'You're like her!' Tom Chapman said. 'Exactly like her . . .' His whole face softened in a smile of gentleness, that was still touched by uncertainty. 'I—I hope you'll be happy with me, girl,' he told this strange young woman who was his daughter. 'We'll have to try and put up with one another . . .'

Her eyes had held, unwavering, upon his face. She had made no move, nor spoken; Stormont, looking at her, had his first pang of doubt. There was compassion in him, understanding her shyness, but also knowing what it would mean to the old man if she turned away from him.

But then, with a sudden movement, she was in her father's arms. Her head pressed against his chest and she was sobbing; and Tom Chapman held her to him, caressing her. In his eyes were the shine of tears, but on his face the most total, unbelieving, blinding happiness Lee Stormont had ever witnessed.

CHAPTER THREE

Jean Lavery, from the vantage point of a second-story window, saw the tall man and the girl coming across the street toward the hotel, and something held her attention on them. She saw the carpetbag, and the traveling dress, and remembered the train whistle she had heard. It was easy to guess the girl had just arrived. She seemed frightened, and Jean felt a pang of sympathy for her.

The jut of the wooden awning cut off view of them as they came up the veranda steps, and Jean forgot them; the man, she had scarcely noticed at all. She returned her attention downstreet, where a momentary flashing of guns, and the running drum of hoofs, seemed already to have been absorbed by the town and forgotten. She wondered again what could have been happening. Then, raising her eyes, she looked across the lower buildings of the town and, against the southern sky, saw the ruddy reflection of thousands of campfires.

A frown of thought worked itself between her fair brows; she stood at the window a moment biting her lower lip uncertainly—careful not to show herself, for she'd removed her dress against the sticky heat and was clad only in a chemise. Her figure, in the washstand mirror, was the mature, full shape of a woman of twenty-five—rather tall for her sex, but well built.

She turned suddenly, and crossed to the bed where her husband lay on his back in trousers and undershirt, asleep, arms behind his head. She pushed the sweaty black curls back from his forehead, then on a decision seated herself by him and laid a hand on his arm. 'Paul,' she said. 'Wake up.'

He groaned a little. His eyes wavered open, he looked at her and then about him at the room. 'Must have dozed off,' he grunted. Seeing the lighted lamp, and the darkness past the open window, he said, 'God, it's late! You had dinner?'

Jean shook her head. 'I didn't want anything. Couldn't have held it.'

'Me either. Damn this heat!' He scrubbed at his scalp. 'What time is it?'

'I don't know. A little after seven, I think. Paul,' she said then, 'I want to talk to you.'

He flopped over onto an elbow; the springs skrealed and the high head of the bed bumped the wall. 'Sure. What about?'

'I've been watching them, down in the street. I never saw so many people in my life. Just listen! And more coming through every minute!'

Paul Lavery looked toward the window, and the racket of voices and wheels and thudding hoofs. 'Poor bastards,' he said condescendingly. 'This isn't much but at least we've got a bed to sleep in tonight. And a roof over our heads.' He lay back and stretched himself again on the hard mattress.

'But I was thinking,' Jean went on, persistent. 'You know there can't be anywhere near enough land to go around, tomorrow. Couldn't we be doing something better than waiting in this hotel?'

'Such as what?' He frowned at her. 'You surely aren't saying you want to go down and camp out there on the line, with that crowd of boomers? After the trouble we had managing to find a room? Don't be ridiculous, Jean!'

'Well . . .' As usual she found herself yielding, reluctantly, doubting the wisdom of her own arguments, weary of the scenes she raised sometimes in crossing him.

'We'll have all morning to find a place in the line. There isn't a thing to worry about.'

'I suppose,' she said, looking down at the hands lying in her lap.

'What's the matter, honey?' Paul touched her hand, then let his fingers move up her bare arm, to the shoulder. 'Worried about tomorrow?'

She shook her head. 'Not really. Looking ahead, I guess—wondering what we'll do if this doesn't work out . . .'

Through the warm hand on her flesh, she could all but feel him go tense. 'What do you mean?' he demanded, his voice roughening with the harshness she had come to know so well. 'It *has* to work out! Our bad luck can't follow us everywhere. This isn't Illinois—it's a new land, where a man has a chance. It's one time they won't be able to hold me down!'

'Paul—' Jean turned on the edge of the bed to face him, determined to put her idea into words however little he might like to hear it. 'I heard someone talking, today, about the townsites that have been laid out. Wouldn't it be a better investment if we could get ourselves a business lot in one of them, instead of going after a quarter section of farm land? You know nothing about farming.'

'What's there to know? I can judge good soil, as well as any of those rubes down in the street. And *you* were raised on a farm, if I wasn't.'

'But—'

'Let me tell you.' He brushed aside her interruption. 'I've got it all figured. Certainly I don't intend winding up as some poverty-stricken farmer! But the trouble with these townsites, none of 'em's worth a damn until the town is built. Only one in twenty will really grow into anything—all depending on how the men upstairs pull the strings. And what happens to the suckers who put all they had on the wrong towns?'

She stared, incredulous. 'You think the whole thing is *fixed*? I can't believe it!'

'Honey, of course it's fixed!' He spoke as

though he were reasoning with a child. 'Everything is, if there's money in it—and millions are going to come out of this business tomorrow. I mean to get my share!

'So, I'm going to pass up the townsites for now, and pick me off a piece of good farm land. That's always a sound investment. I can afford to wait a few months—wait till things have shaken down a bit and we know just which of the new towns is the sure one to back.'

Jean, looking at her husband's handsome face, felt the stir of doubt. She said slowly, 'You're always looking for the sure thing, Paul. Do you really think you'll ever find it?'

His look became stubborn. 'Honey, I've got as good brains as any man I ever met. All I ever needed was a chance. Instead, they've tried to hold me in one small job after another, that had no future—and I won't settle for that! The only way to make a killing is to watch and be ready when the day comes. Well, I've got a hunch tomorrow is my day! The opportunities in this new land are there, for the right man to shape them. You just watch me—and don't worry!'

His eyes had lighted as he talked, whipped to enthusiasm by his own imaginings. But now his sudden awareness of her body, and of her soft flesh under his hand, translated itself into something else. He pulled her roughly down to him.

'Darling!' she murmured in protest, freeing her lips. 'The window—!'

A jerk of his head indicated the offending lamp. She rose and crossed to the dresser where it stood, and bending over the upwash of light she glanced back at her husband, at his flushed face she had always thought so handsome, and the eager waiting look. Then, blowing across the top of the glass chimney into her cupped hand, she plunged the dingy hotel room into blackness.

But when Paul slept again beside her, she lay and stared into the dark, the questions pouring in on her. And she found herself asking, When did I lose faith in him?

A long time ago, she realized—only, she had hidden the secret from herself, guiltily, with passionate denial. Now there was no hiding it any longer. Seven years had been too much, years of listening to his talk that never came to anything; of jobs sought after and then thrown away because they proved to be disappointingly slow roads to advancement. Ignorant about life, and deeply in love, she had had to seek behind his excuses and discover for herself, at last, the real reason for Paul Lavery's failures.

Faith died hard—love, still harder. In a way she was proud of her husband, even yet—his slim good looks, the charm that touched nearly everyone he met and blinded them briefly to the emptiness that lay behind it. Even yet she could not deny his lovemaking and the response it roused in her. But tonight she knew, with clear understanding, that they faced the final test.

She had done all she could. She had accepted Paul's decision to come to this new, raw land, where all doors would be open and where, he assured her, he would find the one golden opportunity that would cancel all the long succession of humdrum jobs and soured ambitions. But this time, if he failed—?

Suddenly Jean was aware that she had been hearing, through the thin partition, a sound of someone weeping. A quick intuition told her it must be the same girl she'd watched from the window. She listened to the lost and lonely sobbing until it gradually ceased, leaving stillness; she wished there were only some sympathy or comfort one could offer the frightened youngster, alone in the adjoining room.

But then, startlingly enough, came something that was almost a twinge of envy. Lying beside her sleeping husband with her hands clenched tight, staring dry-eyed into the darkness, it struck her what a relief and a comfort it really must be, to cry—if a person were so made that she could do it.

* * *

As soon as a place could be found to unhitch

the horses and make camp, Jody Yaeger set to helping his father with the loosened wagon tire. They had no proper tools, and no good way to heat the tire, or water enough for soaking the wheel's sun-shrunken timbers. So, having jacked the axle up as best he could, Yaeger started driving wedges in under the iron, sledging them home with blows of a heavy maul. The sound of the hammering rang strongly across the heat of afternoon, mingled with all the noises around them—the high-pitched talk, the rattle of wheels and bark of dogs, the bawling of a sick baby in the next camp.

Watching his father, admiring the way he handled the heavy sledge and made up with skill what he lacked in bodily strength, Jody was put in mind of the stranger who'd stopped to help them. He asked, without warning, 'Pa, who do you reckon he was?'

Gib Yaeger seemed to understand what his son was talking about. He paused to mop sweat from his face, and look at the job he was doing. 'Wouldn't rightly know, son. I had a feeling he was no land rusher, like the rest of us.'

'Sure nice to lend us a hand . . .'

'One reason I figure he wasn't any boomer. Everybody in this crowd is too excited over gettin' something for themselves. They wouldn't stop long enough to worry about another fellow happening to be in a hole.'

Jody frowned over this, as his father drove another wedge home between rim and tire. '*We* would, Pa,' he protested, finally. 'So I reckon there's others.'

'I reckon.' Satisfied with the job, Yaeger collected his tools and walked over to the wagon and threw them in the box. From his quiet manner he was plainly thinking about the things they'd said. He stood with both hands in the hip pockets of his overalls, looking at the cracked and dusty ground. He nodded soberly.

'Yes, you're right, boy, and I'm wrong. It don't pay to lump people together like that, because all of us are different. Now, this Stormont fellow—I got a feeling he makes the same mistakes. He pegged us for boomers, and so for that reason he didn't like us.'

'Why, he acted real friendly!'

'Later. Not at first. I don't know why he'd feel that way, except there was something about him that looked like he might have been a cowman, once. I guess cowmen never were inclined to like farmers.'

'Why not, Pa?'

The man gave his son a slow grin, and patted his shoulder. 'Maybe they lump us together . . . Well, now, I think that tire will stay on, at least for tomorrow. Help me take the blocks out from under the axle, and we'll have a look at this Cherokee Outlet before your mother's ready to call supper. Before it gets dark, too.'

They had to walk nearly half a mile, picking their way through the congestion of the camps. But then, just as though a line had been drawn with a ruler, the clutter and jam of thousands of people came to an end and out beyond the line was nothing at all. They halted and looked out on all that emptiness, not either of them able to say anything. They had come so far, and staked so much on tomorrow, that it was hard to believe they were at last really looking at the new land.

Day was quickly fading; stars came out as the sky paled and the stretching earth darkened. A couple of other men stood nearby, also staring wordlessly into the growing night, and Yaeger exclaimed suddenly, 'Looks like a fire, out there!'

'The whole Strip's ablaze,' one answered. 'I heard somebody say the military set it. They're burnin' off the grass so we can find the markers easier.'

A trooper, his blue shirt dark with sweat, and a corporal's chevrons on his sleeves, rode slowly past, patrolling the line. Jody watched him open-mouthed, as far as he could make him out in the gathering dusk. He'd never before seen a soldier, up that close.

'What *I* hear,' the second man put in, 'they're tryin' to drive the sooners out. Bet that grass is full of 'em as fleas on a Missouri dawg! What the hell chance has an honest man got?'

'You registered yet?' the first one asked.

Gib Yaeger turned quickly. 'What's that about registering?'

'Why, you got to sign up before you can make the run. They compare signatures later, when you put in for your claim. It's another way to try and lick the sooners.'

'I didn't know anything about this! Where am I supposed to go?'

The man pointed. 'They got booths set up—there's one along here about a quarter mile. If you ain't done it already, you better!'

Yaeger nodded his thanks, and spoke to Jody and they headed in that direction. Sure enough they found the booth—a little clapboard affair, with a couple of officials behind the drop-front counter, working by thin lamplight. They saw the line, too. At the length of it, stretching almost out of sight, and the slow rate it inched forward one man at a time, Gib Yeager shook his head in tired disgust.

'Such foolishness! It won't stop anyone from registering and sneaking onto the Strip afterward . . . Well, if I got to,' he said resignedly, 'I might as well fall in. Can you find your way back?'

'Sure.' Jody almost believed it.

'Tell your mother where I am. I could be here all night, rate this line is moving!'

'Let me stand for you, Pa. At least I can spell you if you get tired.'

'We'll see. Right now you best get on back

so your mother won't worry.'

The wagon was harder to locate than he'd expected. Twice Jody lost his bearings and he became frightened by the strangeness of it all—the raucous noise and the fireglow, the dust that drifted chokingly everywhere. From no place a pair of men, locked in combat, came stumbling into him and they all went down in a tangle. Jody smelled the booze and the sweat and heard the fiercely grunted curses. He broke loose, scrambled to his feet, caught the sudden gleam of a knife blade. He turned and ran from there.

Then, unexpectedly, there was the wagon and his own campfire, a welcome and friendly sight; but no sign of his sister or mother. It was while he stood peering around, wondering where they had got to and already growing a little uneasy, that he saw the boots.

All but that much of the two men was hidden behind the wagon box; but Jody knew what they were up to. His chest swelled with fury. Lord knew his folks had little enough, that they could afford losing any of it to a pair of sneak thieves! Sobering, then, he remembered his pa's revolver. But that, too, was in the wagon—under the seat.

He drew a deep, trembling breath, and started forward.

A few whispered words came to him, the rattle of the endgate dropping open. Now he was beside the big front wheel. As he put his foot to one of the spokes, to lift himself over the edge of the box, a warning shake of the wagon told him one of the prowlers had crawled inside; except for the canvas he might have reached and touched him. Jody swallowed with a dry throat, set his teeth, and stepped up.

On his knees, he groped underneath the seat and found the gun. It was an old Smith & Wesson percussion revolver, refitted for cartridges. Jody had never fired the thing—his pa wouldn't let him. He couldn't even say if it was loaded. Crouching beneath the wagon seat, he used both thumbs to haul back the stiff-working hammer, heard it click and felt the cylinder turn. He scrubbed the palm of his right hand dry against his shirt, and took the gun in it and put his finger on the trigger. Then he crawled forth.

He was climbing to his feet when hands pawed at the canvas and the forward bow was suddenly ripped open. A face appeared—a nondescript, whiskered face. It stared open-mouthed at Jody and Jody stared back. And then, of its own volition, Jody's finger worked and the old gun went off with a roar and a blinding flash.

He was knocked into the wagon bed by the kick of it. He blinked, seeing the hole his bullet had torn in the canvas, hearing the ring of concussion in his ears and the prowler's yelp of terror. The wagon shook convulsively as the man went scrambling out the rear; boots pounded as both of them took for the shadows.

A woman screamed. Dimly he knew it was his mother.

She'd taken Sis and gone over to see that sick baby at the neighboring camp, with a neighborly wish to suggest something for its colicky crying. She'd only been gone a minute, but it had been long enough for the scavengers to light on a deserted wagon camp. When she saw Jody, dazed and white and the gun smoking in his fingers, she began to cry but managed to catch herself. She laid an arm on his shoulder and said, in a queer voice, 'That was a good, brave boy, Jody!'

But she took the gun from him and flung it, hard, into the wagon, as though she couldn't bear the touch of it.

Much later, when he set out to hunt for the registration booth again, Jody carried with him some corn bread and bacon she'd wrapped in a cloth to keep it hot, and a can of black coffee. The booth was just where he'd left it. He had to walk slowly down the line looking at every face before he heard his father calling and saw him, about a third of the way from the end. Gib Yaeger looked awfully tired.

'Here's some grub for you, Pa,' Jody said. 'I'll stand, while you eat.'

'Thanks.' Gib Yaeger, taking the food, peered a long moment into his son's face.

'Everything all right at camp?' he demanded.

'Right as rain.'

But Yaeger continued a trifle longer to stare at the boy, in puzzlement. It was almost as though he'd seen him grow up a little, in something less than an hour.

CHAPTER FOUR

A blank blue sky, a steady scorching wind from the south, a pounding sun that poured its heat on a world night hadn't really cooled—such was this morning of the sixteenth of September, 1893. At the wagon yard on the edge of Caldwell, activity had begun long before sunup. Lee Stormont had ordered a final check of all rolling stock. Once noon came, there would be no letup; the wagons would be rolling, then, day and night—shuttling without pause over the trails of the new Territory.

Tom Chapman, this morning, seemed a younger man than Stormont had ever known him. The nearing deadline seemed unable to affect him; he moved in a kind of daze, and toward eleven o'clock he came where Stormont was examining the underpinnings of a loaded freight wagon and went down on his heels in the dust beside him. Stormont knew before he spoke what was on the man's mind;

he anticipated it with a question.

'How's Lucy?'

Chapman nodded. 'We had breakfast together, at the hotel. I think she likes me, Lee!'

Stormont smiled a little. 'I never knew anyone that didn't.' He saw the shadow that crossed his friend's eyes, then, and he added softly, 'No exceptions, Tom—I mean it. I didn't know her mother, but even there the trouble was something too big for either of you to buck. She must have loved you. She couldn't have helped.'

'I don't know. I guess it was my fault . . .' Tom looked down at his hands. He ground the knuckles of one fist slowly into the other palm. 'I think you understand me better than most men. We're a lot alike—we were meant for one kind of world, and we can't knock the rough edges off to fit into another. It makes me a little scared, Lee. She's so like her mother; will I lose *her*, too? Will I drive her away?'

'Where could she go?'

'There are people of her mother's, back in New Hampshire—distant relatives. They've offered to take her, any time.' His voice tightened. 'Now that I've seen her, and held her in my arms, I reckon it would about kill me if she went!'

Stormont looked into the man's face, seeing there all the basic goodness of him—the real simplicity, despite the bigness of his operations. He said gently, 'Don't worry, Tom. I've got my feeling about Lucy. I think she'll stick.'

Over at the clapboard station an engine was building steam, a half-dozen open cattle cars hooked to it. These cars were already more than half loaded with men, and now Chapman put his hands flat upon his thighs and pushed himself erect. 'I'll have to get along,' he said. 'I won't be seeing her for a long time now, but you'll be in town off and on. Look after her, Lee. Whenever you have a minute.'

'You didn't need to ask me.'

He walked with his boss, across the cinders to the station. A hubbub of noise enveloped the train as men fought to pile into it, to climb the sides and find a precarious perch atop the cars. It was the one scheduled to drop its passengers off at the various townsites along the right of way, where they could stake lots for themselves. Until the signal gun, they faced a bad time—crowded in the close, packed heat like a beef shipment. Stormont managed to get his friend one of the last small spaces available in the stock cars. He was sorry for Tom, but the old man was tough and could take it. Nor would he have considered for a moment letting anyone go through this for him. He would stake his own claim.

As Stormont watched, the engine whistled and amid a din of cheering started slowly away from the station, moving down to the deadline. He saw bottles brandished. Somebody in one of the cars fired off a gun, reckless of the safety of those clinging to the roof.

Stormont returned thoughtfully to his work.

The town was emptying now; dust churned ceaselessly along the wagon trail southward as horsemen and wagons poured toward the line. Presently this tide began to thin. Stormont gave Pete Quilter the long awaited order: 'Have them start hitching up. Soon as the road's clear enough we'll move the wagons on up as close as we can get.' After that, with a moment he could spare, he walked back up the street to the ugly, unpainted hotel.

Strange, how deserted the town was beginning to look. Trash littered the street, papers blew before a stinging, dust-laden wind. Doors stood open, and windows gaped blankly on what had been a scene of ceaseless activity. Yonder he saw that Murray Lenson's big tent had been struck and workmen were rolling it, other men packing card tables and whiskey barrels and gambling equipment into wagons. He saw Lenson himself, walking about with hands shoved in his waistband, shouting orders.

Not for Murray Lenson, he thought, the discomfort of riding a cattle car to stake his own business lot in the Strip. An underling would be paid to do that job, and then relinquish title to his employer. Such wasn't according to the intentions of the men who had planned today's operation, but it was not illegal and there was no way to prevent the fat man from doing it.

The hotel lobby was deserted; the doors along the upper corridor stood open on torn-up and hastily vacated rooms where as many as six boomers had slept in a single bed. After Stormont's knock at Lucy Chapman's door there was no answer for a moment. He identified himself, and at once the bolt snicked back and she opened to him.

She looked much fresher, after a night's rest. Her color was better, the resilience of the very young had worked its simple magic. She smiled as she greeted Stormont, stepping back for him, and he entered, ducking the low doorway. He stood with his hat in his hands.

The contrast of her fresh young beauty against this dreary room struck hard at him.

'Your father's already gone,' he told her. 'And I'll be leaving in a minute. I just wondered if there was anything you wanted.'

'I'll be all right,' she said, and smiled her thanks.

He jerked his head toward the south. 'Maybe you'd like to go down, and watch—'

'No. I'm too thrashed out from yesterday. Besides, I promised not to get in the way. I won't interfere when you're so busy.' She placed a hand upon his arm, impulsively. 'But I do want you to know that I'm sorry, about—

last night. Things look different by daylight, after a good night's sleep. I acted like a baby; I don't know what you must have thought of me!'

'All I thought,' Stormont assured her, 'was how lucky Tom Chapman was! A wonderful man, Lucy! I know it must be strange, having to accept a father that you can't remember ever seeing before, but—give him a chance. Take him as he is, they don't come any better. And the one thing he wants, now, is to make you learn to love him!'

'I think I do, already,' she said, and Stormont thanked her with the pressure of his hand in hers.

'Sorry you have to stay here, alone,' he said then. 'Stick close to the hotel; the Binghams are good people—they'll do anything you ask. And you'll be seeing me, off and on.'

'I'll be perfectly all right,' the girl insisted; and he took the image of her, and the sound of her voice, with him as he left the building and turned downstreet again, moving hurriedly now with the growing pressure of speeding time.

Part of the wagons were hitched and lined out, ready for the road. Stormont's blue roan was waiting. He checked the cinch, and swung astride. The road to the south lay empty and blown clear of the last lifted dust. He raised himself in stirrups, flung his arm forward in the signal to roll. The yells of the teamsters and the crack of the whips echoed his shout; mules hit their collars and ponderously the big, weighted rigs went into motion.

Stormont waited until the lead wagons had lurched across the flat and stretched out along the road; then, knowing he could trust Pete Quilter to keep them coming, he spurred ahead along the line. Wind whipped the canvas, in a steady flutter of rifle shots. He overtook and passed the lead wagon and, reaching a slight rise in the nearly level land, held up and there twisted about to signal the driver. 'Hold 'em here,' he said, and the man nodded and pulled the teams to a halt, while the word went back. Stormont turned and stared at the scene spread out ahead of him.

A steady tide of sound beat toward him on the wind. With ten minutes to go, the boomers were already crowding the starting line. They made a solidly packed mass that stretched beyond sight in both directions. In the forefront, horsemen were jockeying for position—a constant shifting that was carried back through the body of the surging, frenzied mob. Behind ranged the wheeled vehicles, light wagons of every description, stripped down to the running gear in the interests of speed. Here and there a prairie schooner lifted its canvas above the rest, but most of the boomers had known better than to try making the run with that kind of a handicap. Mostly the clumsy rigs stood stripped of their teams and abandoned, amid the vacated camps and smoldering cookfires.

Out in front, facing the pack, a thin line of troopers stood with rifles grounded and waiting to pass the signal. Beyond lay the Strip, peaceful in these last moments before the assault, under a sky blackened by grass-fire smoke and scorched by the blistering wind.

A buckboard came along the road from town, outside wheels jolting over weedy ground in order to clear the line of freight wagons. Turning, Stormont saw three persons crowded onto the seat; it was George Bingham handling the reins, and the one squeezed in between him and his wife was Lucy Chapman. Both women carried sunshades, and the hotelman was swearing jovially as he maneuvered his team. All three were laughing over the way the buckboard jostled and tossed them about.

Bingham pulled to a halt and pushed the hat back from his bald head; a sudden hush fell on the people in the buckboard. Seeing Stormont, the hotelman grinned and indicated the girl beside him. 'We convinced her this was a sight none of us'd ever get another chance at. Bundled her in and brung her for a look. Ain't sorry, are you, honey?'

Lucy breathed quickly, 'Oh, no!' She had turned completely solemn; her eyes were wide as they gazed, absorbed, over that panorama spread out before her.

Bingham pointed with his whip toward the engine and train of loaded cars. 'Your daddy's down there somewhere, girl. He'll be one of the first inside the new Territory. What time is it, Nettie?'

His wife, a plump and handsome woman of forty, ducked her head to examine the small gold watch pinned at her bosom. 'Three minutes to go,' she said.

A subtle change had come over the waiting crowd. Even from here it could be felt. The line appeared to stiffen, its voice lifted to a new note of hysteria. The soldiers out front had their rifles lifted now and ready to throw them to their shoulders. Stormont suddenly realized he shared the tightening of suspense, and frowned thinking, You've got nothing to get excited over! He made his hands loosen on the reins.

When the signal came, he couldn't even hear the crack of the guns. He saw muzzle smoke leap from the rifles, and then the roar of the crowd swelling to a scream and the tide of horsemen sweeping forward. Stormont found himself lifted in the stirrups. Through a quickly raised canopy of hoof-churned dust, he could see the front of the wave break as faster horses took the lead. More slowly, the buckboards and wagons and prairie schooners lurched forward. Last of all, the whistle of the diamond-stack locomotive let go in a long blast and a white plume of steam, and the drive wheels caught the rails; men clinging to cattle car roofs and grab irons emptied their six-shooters wildly at the sky.

In a great, convulsive motion, that mass of humanity went pouring out into the empty, waiting land.

Stormont turned in the stirrups to yell at his drivers: 'Here we go!' He waved them forward with a wide sweep of his hat. Whips cracked, drivers whooped up their teams. With the big wheels already turning and lifting powder-dry dust for the wind to fling away, Stormont squared around and settled into the leather, dragging on his hat again.

A kick of the spurs sent the roan forward. He eased into a steady lope and, with the line of freight rigs lumbering behind him, took the rutted freight trail in the wake of the stampede.

The scattered camps were forgotten now, abandoned. Already, along the starting line, those the rush had left behind were milling aimlessly in a dazed letdown of tension. Stormont had to shout at them to clear the trail: 'Watch these wagons! If you don't want to get flattened, move out of the way!' He pushed through the mob, and then he was in the clear and the trail led south.

The blistering wind was in his face, smoke stung his nostrils. All about and ahead was movement, scattered wide across what had been, five minutes before, an empty plain.

Already, here and there, men were down from their horses, driving stakes and making a mad scramble to find the corner markers. He saw, too, the first signs of tragedy. Here, a horse had stumbled and fallen with its rider. Farther on, two wagons had met in a reckless side-swiping collision and were a tangle of horses and wreckage and motionless bodies. He didn't stop for anything. His sole concern was the wagon trail, to see that it was clear so the loaded freight rigs would have passage.

The smoke was growing worse. He could see a black billow of it ahead and he eyed it with concern. It looked as though the whole prairie was burning. If the supply wagons kept to the trail they should not be in great danger, but the mules could panic. Already the roan was fidgeting under the smarting sting; he settled it, with a firm hand. And going over a slight hump of prairie ground he saw the fire.

Close at his right hand the ground dropped away into a brushy ravine, and along that funnel the flames were crackling before the push of the wind. Trail-side weeds were burning, in places. The roan made a sound of fear as it saw, but he wouldn't let it bolt. The fire would scarcely sweep near enough to menace the wagon road itself; but the smoke that lay here was like a punishing, eye-smarting pall.

It thinned briefly as swirling air currents tore it apart and gave him the briefest glimpse of a light wagon some fifty yards ahead. The team horses, gone crazy, were fighting the reins; he saw the wagon jerked crazily back and forth behind the rearing and squealing horses. Just as the smoke curtain dropped again, he saw the lift of a rear wheel and the rig flipped neatly over.

Seconds later he reached the spot where the wagon had left the road; he could hear it, rumbling over and over down into the ravine, while the horses screamed their pain and terror. A man had been flung clear by the crash and was on his hands and knees in black, burned weeds beside the trail. As Stormont spurred up he was shaking his head, dazedly.

'You all right?' Stormont had to repeat it, leaning from the saddle. The man's head lifted groggily; he brought his dazed eyes to focus. 'Yeah,' he muttered. 'Yeah, I guess so.' He was a youngish fellow, who didn't look as though he had the wrists to manage a bolting team. He came onto his knees, and ran an arm across his forehead, smearing it with black ash and sweat.

Stormont looked over into the steep-walled ravine, but there was little to be seen but the billowing curtain of smoke, and the red pattern of the fire licking along the limbs of brush and skimpy trees. '*That* rig's lost,' he said, shortly.

The man nodded again. He groped for Stormont's stirrup and used it to haul himself to his feet. He looked around him and exclaimed suddenly, 'Jean—!'

Stormont leaned closer. 'What?'

'My wife. I don't— She must not have jumped clear!'

'You mean you had a woman in that rig?' Stormont felt the ugly knotting start inside. 'Why the hell couldn't you say so?' Without hesitation he pulled the rein and gave his horse a kick that jerked the stirrup out of the man's hand. The roan tried to balk but Stormont drove it down into drifting, red-shot smoke. The wagon had torn a plain trail, through weeds and burning brush. Stones rattled and the roan nearly lost its footing; it braced its legs and took the drop in a slide. Something was thrashing down there—one of the wagon team. Then, almost on top of it, he saw the rig.

It was badly smashed; it lay upside down at the bottom of the draw, one wheel still spinning. The sickness in Stormont's guts made his limbs tremble, but he forced himself to pull rein and examine what was left of the wagon. Its horses lay in a tangle of harness, one motionless but the other fighting to get free; that was the thrashing sound he had heard, above the crackling of the fire all around him. Reluctantly, Stormont placed a hand upon the upturned body of the rig. He supposed he would have to turn it over, and uncover what lay beneath the wreckage . . .

Then, at a sound, his head lifted and on the other side of the wagon he saw the woman, on her knees. She was panting, struggling with something she was trying to pull from under the wreck; when Stormont shouted at her she glanced at him briefly through the swirl of smoke. He saw her face was bruised and on one arm a long scratch was bleeding. Her clothing had been torn and her fair hair tangled and disarrayed, but she seemed more dazed than hurt.

She returned to her burrowing, and with a curse Stormont forced his mount to scramble around the pile-up. Flaming brands were floating about them. He reached from the saddle and seized the woman by an arm, to haul her to her feet. 'You can't stay here!' he exclaimed. 'Do you want to burn up?'

'Let go of me!' She struck at him, hard, with her fist; surprised, Stormont let go and she stumbled back against the wagon. 'I'm going to save this suitcase!'

Almost without thinking he was out of saddle, the rounded pebbles of the dry wash clattering and turning under his boots. A wave of hot smoke hit his lungs just then and he doubled, coughing. With tears blurring and smarting he groped, got his hands under the edge of the smashed wagon box and raised it.

He could hear the woman working, beside him. She staggered, nearly falling, as the trapped suitcase pulled free; Stormont dropped the edge of the wagon box and turned to her.

The suitcase was a cheap straw affair, heavy and bulging with its contents. It had been tied with a rope, which was a good thing because the handle had been ripped off and one side split in the wreck. He took it from her and asked, 'Can you ride a horse?'

'Certainly. But—'

He pushed her toward the roan. 'Then mount up. Hurry!'

She was hampered by her long skirt, and shock made her tremble badly. But with a boost from Stormont she managed to swing astride the roan, and then the man tossed the battered suitcase up to her and made a quick tie with a saddle string holding it in place. He said, 'Now, get out of here!' and gave the roan a slap on the rump to start it.

The woman tried to say, 'But what about you?' The horse, frightened by the fire and stinging smoke, leaped ahead, with a lurch that almost threw her off. Stormont was already turning back to look at the team of the wrecked wagon.

One of the horses, he saw immediately, was dead, its neck twisted at a gruesome angle; but the other had fared better and was thrashing wildly to escape. Stormont spoke to it as he got out his pocket knife. He worked quickly, slashing the tangled harness. When the horse struggled to its feet he grabbed the head stall and flung himself upon its bare back.

He put the animal at the loose-graveled bank and after a poor first try the panicked horse got its hoofs in and managed to scramble out of the trap of smoke and wind-pushed fire. The couple were waiting for him, the woman still clinging to the roan's saddle, her husband holding its reins to steady it. 'That was a close one,' Stormont grunted, swabbing his sweaty face upon a sleeve. 'You could both have been killed!'

The man did not seem particularly grateful that they hadn't. 'What do we do now?' he demanded. His wife was quick to correct him, however. Impulsively she stretched a hand to their benefactor.

'We'll make out,' she said, and smiled, a little wanly. 'We're thankful for your help.'

He took the hand. It was strong and graceful, though dirty and scratched now from the accident. It made him look more closely at the woman and he saw that she was like her hand—still young, and with a strength in her that you could sense. Her fair hair was tangled and disarrayed, but he knew that she was a handsome girl and her blue eyes had a directness that he liked. Her husband, on the contrary, showed a petulant obstinacy that hinted of weakness.

Stormont looked around him, getting his bearings. 'If you folks are thinking of staking a claim, you've not got much time! That roan will carry double,' he told the man. 'Get up behind your wife. I know this country pretty well. Maybe I can put you on some good-enough land.'

The dark-haired man only stared at him. It was the woman who jarred her husband into motion. 'Hurry, Paul! Do what he says.' Stormont waited long enough to see the man moving awkwardly to climb up in back of her—no horseman, obviously, and not a farmer either to judge by his appearance.

'Follow me,' he said, and used the spurs.

CHAPTER FIVE

The wagon-team horse didn't like having a rider up, but Stormont settled it into a steady gait—one he knew the roan, even with a double burden, could keep up with. They turned away from the trail, and the warm air lost some of that irritating smoke tang as they left the burn-out in the ravine behind them.

The rush of stampeding hoofs had struck this section and passed, but as yet the fires hadn't touched it. They entered a belt of leaf-stripped trees and Stormont heard distantly a spatter of gunplay that ended as quickly as it began; he thought, Somebody's settling an argument! A wild turkey dropped out of one of the trees and went flopping away. Then the trees cleared and fell back. On a brown stretch of grass, yonder, a man stood beside a lathered horse, a flag fluttering from the end of the stake he'd driven. A gun winked sunlight in his hand; he kept a cautious watch until the riders had gone by and dwindled from sight.

Stormont pointed between a couple of low hills, and after another ten minutes came out onto a wedge of grassland that fell gently toward a timbered bottom. He saw no movement, and decided he'd guessed right: To the north a sandstone ledge would have deflected the first wave, just enough to miss the good bottomland soil beyond. Stormont pulled his horse in and waited for the roan to come up. He swung an arm, pointing. 'You'll find no better,' he said. 'It's yours for the taking . . .'

The roan had been hard used. It stood under its double burden with head hanging and sweat glistening and running down its legs. The man said dubiously, 'Looks all right, I guess.'

'It looks wonderful!' his wife exclaimed. 'Trees for a wind break and for fuel, and this north slope to protect it in winter. It will be good, rich land.'

Stormont looked at her, thinking, She knows the score, if her husband doesn't! What he said was, 'You have your flag ready?' The man nodded. 'Then go stake it!'

They took the slope at an easier pace, and

leveled out at the foot of it where cottonwood and elm cast small pools of shade. The woman's husband had produced a length of stick with a cloth tied to its end. Seeing him about to drop down from the roan's back, Stormont said quickly, 'Not yet. Let's find the corner marker.' It wasn't easy to locate, in the high dry grass. They quartered across the bottoms, searching; it was the woman who discovered the little mound with its concrete slab.

Stormont jumped down and trampled the yellow stubble under his boots, making the marker easier to read. 'That's what I was afraid might happen,' he grunted. 'A school section! If you'd tried to claim it you'd have wasted your chance. Go across the line and drop your stake. That will give you the best quarter of land anyway. There's water beyond those cottonwoods—the horses can smell it already. If it's running this time of year, it's a stream that won't ever go dry on you.'

The man slid down across the roan's rump, without a word, and went to drive his stake into the unbroken sod. Stormont looked at the woman, and saw the gratitude in her eyes. 'Thank you,' she said simply.

He shrugged. 'No reason to.' He stepped over beside the roan then, and lifted his hands to her. 'Help you down?'

She was firmly built, strong. For a moment after he had set her on her feet they stood with his hands at her waist and her fingers resting along his forearms. A sleeve of her dress was torn and the shoulder showed creamy white beneath. Stormont took his eyes away from that. As he stepped back, he caught again the dull gleam of gold on her left hand.

'I was glad to be of help,' he told her. 'Mrs.—'

'Lavery,' she supplied, quickly. 'My name is Jean. My husband—'

He nodded. 'Paul—I heard you say it. Lee Stormont's my name.'

'We're happy to know you.'

The formality, under such circumstances, seemed a little out of place. Stormont moved to his roan and untied the battered suitcase from the saddle and set it on the grass. He laid a hand on the mount's sweat-shiny neck. 'Needs a drink,' he said. 'I'll see if I can find him one yonder. Then I'll have to ride.' He had taken a couple of steps before he turned back, dissatisfied. The woman stood as he had left her, in her torn dress, the old suitcase at her feet. Her fair hair, hopelessly tangled, was blowing in the steady, scorching wind. She had put up one hand and was trying to order it, to smooth it against her neck with a gesture that was so wholly feminine he forgot the dirt and the blood.

Yonder Paul Lavery was squatting on his ankles, running a handful of soil through his fingers and letting the wind carry it off in long streamers. His expression was brooding and balky. 'You think you'll be all right?' Stormont asked the woman. 'You haven't any tools—anything at all.'

'We'll make out.'

He said bluntly, 'At least I hope you have a gun.'

If he expected to startle her, he did not succeed. 'In there,' she said, and touched the suitcase with a toe. Her matter-of-fact answer reassured him a little.

'I'm glad to hear that,' he said. 'This is good land. You may find yourself having to fight for it.'

'I can usually take care of myself!' Paul Lavery said. He had stood up and was facing them, a sullen look on his spoiled, good-looking face. His manner was a dismissal, and Stormont stiffened a little.

'Good!' he said curtly. 'If there should be any way I can help, look me up at Comanche townsite. It lies about eleven miles south and west—it's where you'll be filing your claim. I'll be headquartering there. Leave a word and it will reach me.'

'Thank you,' said the woman. 'We'll remember.'

'Best of luck.'

Abruptly he turned and, leading the horse, walked across the dry earth to the stream that ran thinly through a pebbled creek bed, beyond the cottonwoods.

As he stood letting the roan have its drink, a couple of horses came out of the brush and up to the other bank. They looked like plow horses, but there were saddles on them; in surprise Stormont recognized the gaunt animals, the same moment that he saw it was Jody Yaeger who rode one and led the other by the reins. The boy knew him, too, and gave a whoop and sent the horses splashing through the tiny trickle of water. He looked tired but aglow with excitement.

'Gee, Mr. Stormont!' he cried. 'Never thought we'd see *you* again, in all this mess! Is this your claim? We got the next quarter, east. Gee!'

Stormont smiled, and shook his head. 'Not my claim, Jody. I helped a couple of people stake it—the Laverys, yonder. You'll like them.'

Jody looked disappointed. 'Aw, that's too bad! I thought we'd be neighbors. Whyn't you takin' any land, Mr. Stormont?'

'It's a long story, Jody—one you probably wouldn't understand . . .'

'Well, I better be riding. I'm on my way to fetch the wagon.'

The horses had been drinking while they talked. Now Jody kicked his heels against the ribs of the gaunt animal that loomed so tall under him, and rode off northward at a shambling gait. Stormont watched him go, afterward checking the cinch on the roan and mounting up. He lifted to a lope, and swung again in the direction of the freight road.

The sorrel was a speedy animal, but Bill Ivy deliberately held it back, knowing—if some others did not—the folly of trying to race a horse over this treacherous prairie. The animal protested when the rest of the pack got the lead in those first thundering moments. It fought the reins, trying to get the bit between its teeth and streak ahead. Bill Ivy grinned, seeing the sorrel's spirit; but he kept the reins tight, willing to eat dust while the yipping, yelling fools around him competed to kill themselves and their horses.

He saw a fine, long-legged buckskin just in front of him take a dog hole and go crashing, spilling its crazy rider into the dust and the hoofs that made the earth quake under their pounding. He had been expecting that to happen and was able to swerve aside and narrowly miss a pile-up. One down! he thought, dryly, and forgot the matter.

He lost more of the competition where a dry stream bed, lined with a few scrubby willows and cottonwoods, suddenly opened across the line of the race. Some men tried to plow straight through and piled up in the brush. Others, who got past that, floundered when their horses struck the loose, dry sand. Bill heard horses squeal as they went down; he heard men yell and curse, and one horrible, choked-off scream when a rider was caught under the crushing weight of his mount. He slogged ahead, taking the treacherous crossing in stride. When he topped out on the opposite bank, still going, the pack had considerably thinned and the dust pall was eased enough that a man could breathe and even see a few hundred feet ahead of him now.

Sight was one thing Bill didn't need to depend on. He could have run this course blindfolded or in the dead of night, if necessary. Just ahead the ground began to rise, shaping up into the flank of a long, barren hill. He bore over, lifting with the spur of ground instead of swinging to stay with the level. Precisely where he knew it would be, he hit a dim trail and let this take him across the hump and along the opposite flank of the ridge, to drop down at last through a thicket of wild plum—leafless now—and so into the head of a long, curving trough.

Suddenly he was alone. A coyote went slinking through the grass at a prowling run; the animals of the prairie, at least, knew that something strange and wrong had hit their empty land.

He glanced across his shoulder, saw he'd lost the pack for a moment. He spurred ahead.

He hit a fork of Pecan Creek, finding it little more than a dark dampness centering its sandy bed. Minutes later he reached the branching, and beyond lay the level acreage of pasture land which he had picked for his claim. Once this had been a cow camp, a substantial layout of sod buildings and corrals and feed pens. He'd wintered here, a deep, cold winter—lying around a stove, eating and sleeping and reading dog-eared magazines and going out to buck the drifts and tail-up cattle that had got too deep into the piling snow. It had been a pleasant, lonely, lazy winter. But now the buildings were gone with little trace-destroyed by order of the Army, along with all other permanent improvements the Cherokee Strip cattlemen had built. The grass grew rank and parched, and the scorching wind ran across it in waves of light and dark, beneath the brassy sky.

Bill rode straight in, directly to the surveyor's mound which he'd located yesterday. He slid his toe out of stirrup and stepped down, leaning to pull the flagged, sharpened stake which was thrust into his boot top. Carrying this, he walked over to the mound. He was directly on top of it before he stopped, gone suddenly still and unmoving.

Someone's stake and flag already thrust from the little hole sunk at the southeast corner of the monument. Bill Ivry looked at it, for a long moment. There was no sound—nothing but the faint stirring of the flag, as the currents of air moved here along the nearly dry creek bed. But inside Bill Ivy a storm of fury began and quickly built, and suddenly with a smothering curse he reached and whipped that offending stake-and-flag from the hole and flung them aside. And only then did he see the figure standing spread-legged in the shadow of a tree yonder, a horse tethered just beyond.

The two stood for a long minute, neither speaking. The hot wind pulled at them, and rattled paper-dry leaves in treeheads along the creek. Shaded by his hat, there was not much to be seen of the second man's face except a scurf of unshaved whiskers; but his eyes were sharp coals, burning just below the sweated brim. Meeting his stare, Bill Ivy dropped the stake he had brought with him, freeing his right hand. He flexed the fingers of that hand, slowly, as though to work stiffness out of them.

The other man spoke, and his voice was heavy and edged with mockery. 'You're a little late . . .'

Measuring him, Bill took his time answering. 'Could be,' he suggested, and his voice was quiet, 'that you're a little soon.'

He saw the other stiffen. 'Chew it finer.'

Bill Ivy's glance had moved past him. 'Is that your bronc I see yonder?'

'Could be.' The man did not turn to see.

'Not a sign of sweat on him,' Bill remarked. 'That animal ain't been ridden anywhere. Not this morning.'

The other's height seemed to contract, subtly; he merely lowered himself slightly, into a crouch. The movement made the gun at his hip thrust its handle out from his body at a ready angle.

'This is a nice piece of land,' the sooner remarked, his lips scarcely moving. 'It belongs to him that can hold it.'

'You want a try?'

'Give the word.'

The wind leaped stronger, rippling the sweaty shirts against their bodies and flipping the brims of their hats. Then the sooner started his draw; and the very instant his hand started toward the holster, Bill Ivy was ready with an answering move.

He lunged aside as he drew, not knowing how fast the other man would be. Actually he was very slow, and Bill had plenty of time. The gun came into his hand, his finger was through the trigger guard and squeezing even before that other six-shooter more than cleared the top of the holster. Bill shot, then a second time. The explosions were thin and flat against the heat and the wind. They knocked the sooner back; his head dropped and the hat fell from it, and he went down in a sideward crumple. He was dead before he hit.

Bill looked at him, feeling nothing at all. He looked at the smoking muzzle of his gun, and used it to push the hat back on his head; then he wiped his mouth on his sleeve, and shoved the gun away.

His throat was suddenly dry. He turned to his horse and got the canteen slung to the saddlehorn, and unstoppered it. He was surprised to find his fingers shook a little. He took a long pull at the tepid water, and screwed the lid on again and let it fall to the end of its canvas strap. Only after that did he walk over and take a look at the body of the man he had killed.

'Damn' sooner!' he grunted, and touched the body with his toe; it gave, limply.

Suddenly he became aware of the thunder of the rush, approaching; belatedly it occurred to him he hadn't staked the claim for which he'd done a killing. He proceeded to do it.

* * *

The thunder had passed. The pall of raised dust had shaken out in the wake of the run and slowly settled; it no longer stood against the sky. The great event was ended. In another sense, it had only begun.

On every quarter section of this land, now, men were already making the first moves to tame the wildness out of it—unloading their belongings, breaking out shovels to begin the digging of wells. Others had brought a new wildness of their own. Lee Stormont, riding out of a clump of leafless pecans that lined a stream bed, saw two men crouched over a disputed marker—not talking or arguing, merely staring at each other while their hands hovered near their guns. He sensed murder in the air and rode wide; and he didn't look back.

There in the pecans he'd seen something else—a body dangling at rope's end from an outthrust limb, and not yet stiff. He'd thought, dryly, One sooner less! and gone on without a second look at the distorted face and staring eyes. He felt no shock or surprise at anything. It was all as he had known it would be—an unlovely spectacle of human greed.

Stoically, he told himself he would do his job for Tom Chapman and once it was done he'd he free to leave, and not have to see any more of what was happening to this Cherokee Outlet.

The big freight wagons were rolling on schedule now—these first, in an unending stream that had to bring the new Territory the supplies its thousands of inhabitants would be needing. The vanguard might expect to reach Comanche townsite sometime after dark. Despite his own biting curiosity to know what was going on down there, and how Tom had made out, Stormont wouldn't make it today. His job was to keep the wagons moving, and the trail clear.

The grass fires had swept on, leaving blackened stubble and ashes that rose, chokingly, to settle on a man's skin and eat at his eyes like lye; the constant wind, an oven blast, dried out the juices in him. Grimly Stormont went on ranging up and down the trail, keeping the wagons spaced, guarding against a breakdown in delivery. At places the ruts were blocked with splintered wagons abandoned by the stampeders, and bodies of horses dropped from exhaustion and already beginning to bloat under the smashing sun. Wherever these couldn't be hauled away to clear the track, the wagons had to pull wide for a detour through prairie stubble.

With the waning afternoon, too, there began to be another hazard; for now they met the first straggle of returning land rushers—those who'd been too slow, or too inept with a gun or lacking in brass and nerve to nail down claims for themselves. Their numbers increased by the moment until they were a slow churning stream; and more than once Stormont saw the speculative, lip-licking stares that were turned on the big freight wagons.

All that wealth of canvas-topped supplies could set thoughts to working, in the heads of men empty-handed from the run. Stormont had foreseen as much, and was glad of the orders he'd issued for every driver and his swamper to carry a gun and keep it displayed in plain sight. Right now, the danger was mostly potential. Later the gangs would begin to take form. And when they did, the freight rigs and their cargoes would face a real menace . . .

The sun was dragging low, now, reddened and swollen by long layers of drifting smoke haze. Riding toward Caldwell, he met a familiar-looking buckboard; he reined in as George Bingham, the hotelkeeper, halted his team. Stormont's face, caked with sweat and dust and blackened by soot, was like a stiff mask as he demanded, 'Where are *you* bound for?'

Bingham grinned a little sheepishly. 'The Strip,' he admitted. 'Figured I was going to sit this one out, but—well, the old town looks a little empty. So I thought I'd take a look at this Comanche; if it looks good and I can get me a piece of ground reasonable, I might even think about moving my business down there. Been ashamed of that rattletrap I call a hotel, since the day I bought it in!'

'Where's Miss Chapman?'

'Oh, she's staying with Nettie. She's going to be all right.' He nodded, sobering. 'I really mean that, Lee. I don't think Tom has anything to worry about. She's a fine little girl.' He added, looking closely at the other man, 'But I don't suppose that's telling you anything you hadn't already noticed . . .'

Stormont was slow to catch his meaning, and when he did he stared. 'A little girl is exactly what she is! Why, I must be at least ten–twelve years older. You needn't start getting notions!'

'I won't,' the hotelman promised. 'But there's going to be a lucky young gent come along some day!' He nodded again, and winked, and clucked to his horses.

Lee Stormont let the buckboard roll past. He frowned, thinking a moment of what Bingham had said. He shook his head and muttered, aloud, 'That's crazy!'

* * *

A strange silence hung over Caldwell. The town was slowly returning to life; defeated land rushers were streaming back through, some of them making camp, others merely wandering aimlessly about the streets. All the excitement of the preceding days was gone. Even the drunks and the kids were subdued now.

But at the Chapman wagon yard, work continued. During the day, more boxcars had been brought into the station siding, and sweating crews were hustling freight into the big wagons, getting teams into harness. Stormont found a pile of manifests waiting to be checked and cleared. By the time he finished, shadows were stretching long across the Kansas prairie and the town's lamps were being lighted. He made a final routine check at the telegraph office but found no messages; his part of this day's work was done.

He cleaned up at the washbench, taking his time about it, and then walked up to the hotel for something to eat. The streets were still, in the dusk. There was a litter of trash in the vacant lot where Murray Lenson's saloon tent had stood, and papers and bottles clogged the gutters. The hotel lobby was as empty as the rest of the town. Nettie Bingham, behind the desk sorting mail, looked up with real relief as Stormont entered.

'Another face besides my own!' she exclaimed. 'Are you spending the night with us, Lee? You can sure have the pick of rooms!'

He shook his head. 'I'll have to pull out again. I was looking for something to eat.' He nodded toward the darkened dining room. 'But it appears you aren't serving.'

'I'll serve you myself! No trouble at all.' Lifting the drop leaf she came around from behind the desk. Stormont followed her as she bustled into the dining room, lighting bracket lamps and chasing out the shadows. 'Not much of a menu tonight,' she told him over her shoulder. 'But name it and I'll see if we can dig it up.'

Stormont hung his hat, and dropped into a chair at one of the oilcloth-covered tables. 'Whatever you have in the kitchen. I'm too tired to quibble.'

'How about beef and potatoes? Got some nice roasting ears, too.'

'And a quart of coffee, neat? Sounds wonderful.' He added: 'I saw George, heading for the Strip. Talked like he was planning to make a move.'

'The last week or two have spoiled him for Caldwell, I'm afraid,' Nettie admitted, wagging her head. 'He'd forgotten, until this afternoon, just how dull it can be here. Was it pretty wild, Lee—the run?'

'Wild enough.' He shook his head. 'I'll never understand the mind that could think up an operation like that one! They'd have done better to draw names out of a hat. There's men and horses lying dead on that prairie tonight that needn't have been there. And there'll be more! Probably half the men that managed to stake a claim will lose it in front of a gun, before daylight!'

Nettie Bingham, standing beside him, laid a hand on his shoulder, an understanding gesture. 'You're thrashed out. Nothing looks good to you. You sit there and relax while I go stir up that cook.'

She went into the kitchen, and he was alone. Legs stretched under the table, shoulders slack with weariness, he brought out materials and built a cigarette. He was tapering and twisting it into shape when there was a step in the lobby doorway; glancing up, he saw Lucy Chapman.

She looked very young and very charming, standing there; she had not expected to see him and she flushed with pleasure and surprise. As she came forward Stormont got to his feet, saying, 'You're just in time to join me. I'll tell Nettie.'

'You don't need to,' the hotelman's wife said, coming in from the kitchen with her hands bristling with silverware. 'You sit right down, honey,' she told the girl. 'I'll set an extra place.

'Thank you,' said Lucy. 'I *am* hungry.'

When he had pulled out a chair for her and then reseated himself, Lee Stormont found an odd reticence settling on him; he wondered at its cause, then realized it had something to do with George Bingham's talk, and with the looks that Nettie bent upon the two of them as she bustled about setting out plates and water glasses and napkins. He thought, with some irritation. They're a couple of matchmaking old women! Despite himself, they had succeeded in making him conscious of Lucy Chapman as a young, sweet, and desirable person.

By contrast with her fresh charm, he felt used and as old as time.

'You're looking well, this evening,' he said. 'Got over your trip?' And as she nodded, dimpling: 'Kind of lonesome, though, for you?'

'Mrs. Bingham's been wonderful.' Her brows, that were shaped like delicate wings, drew together in a frown. 'But you look awfully tired, Lee.'

'I am,' he admitted. 'It's been a long day . . . and this is only the beginning.'

He told her, then, a little of what the run had been like. There were many things, of course, he made no mention of, but even so it was an exciting story and Lucy heard it through in silent, rapt attention. Before he finished, Mrs. Bingham brought in plates heaped high with meat and potatoes and gravy and biscuits, corn dripping melted butter, and a pot of black coffee.

Lucy wanted to know, finally, 'Have you seen my father?'

'No, but I've had word. He got his lot at Comanche, all right. That town will grow up overnight, Lucy. In no time at all he'll be sending for you to join him in your new home.'

'How wonderful.' But she spoke without real enthusiasm, and her voice held a shade of doubt that made Stormont reach a hand across the table to cover her own.

'You'll like it,' he assured her earnestly. 'I'm certain you will. It's new, and it's going to be kind of wild for a time; but that will change. And so will you! I hope you'll try to believe that, anyway—for Tom's sake.'

She smiled, then. 'I'm not afraid,' she said. 'Really! I was a little at first—coming here. But I have friends already. You, and the Binghams . . . I understand they're moving to Comanche. I hope they are. I'd like Nettie for a neighbor.'

For no reason, Stormont found himself thinking then of that other woman, Jean Lavery. And the Yaegers. They were people he was sure Lucy would like.

His meal finished, he rose and got his hat off the wall hook. The girl said, 'You're leaving me?'

'Afraid so. My job in this town is finished, and there's plenty of work waiting in the Strip.' She stretched out her hand and he paused beside the table, holding it a moment as he looked down at her. 'I'll tell your dad I saw you—and that you're prettier than ever. I think this country is going to agree with you.'

He wished, as he left her and walked out of the hotel, that he could really be sure of it . . .

The last light had gone from the prairie and the stars stretched their mesh from one low horizon to the other. Stormont walked through silent streets to the wagon yard at the edge of town, and there made short work of collecting his few belongings and tying them into a bundle. A skinner was working by lantern light, making a last check on wagon and teams. Stormont walked over. 'Pulling out? I'll pile in the back.'

He dumped his stuff aboard, swung up the high wheel and climbed in over the tailgate. The wagon was loaded with bags of grain, and he made a comfortable bed for himself without difficulty.

The jolting of the wheels over prairie sod was not enough to keep him long awake.

CHAPTER SIX

The tireless wind that parched this land through the day had died completely, now. Gib Yaeger, standing in thickening dusk while the cooler breath of night dried the sweat on his shirt, looked out across the prairie and watched campfires begin to glow. They looked to him like stars flung to the earth, and they all marked homestead claims, like this one, where there'd been only empty prairie when the sun rose.

It had been a day of danger and problems. Scarcely had he got his well dug, and a little windfall timber gathered to be axed into kindling, when Martha and the children had arrived with the wagon and a warning of grass fires nearing on the shifting wind. The plow had come down from its lashings on the side of the wagon box, then, and Yaeger had spent an hour running hasty furrows around the site of their camp, hoping these would serve as a fire break. Smoke had swirled nearer, stinging the throat and darkening the sky, and at a shout from Jody he'd looked up once to watch a doe and her fawns move in a panic across the grass.

But the wind must have shifted again; for the fire came no closer, though the cloud of smoke had stained the sky along the horizon for hours. So, that was one danger past. But not the only one.

In the stillness, a thin shred of human voices came to him now from a hollow a little to the south, where sparks from a fire streamed like a banner in the night. Gib Yaeger's eyes hardened. The two men—brothers, from the look of them—had been camped there for the past four hours. When Yaeger went to them with a warning that the claim was already taken, they'd only stared at him from flat, expressionless faces, with an insolence that was like a threat.

Yaeger knew it was a threat he'd have to meet; and this might as well be the time.

He was a man of peace, but there was no hesitation about him now as he walked over to the wagon and took his old Smith & Wesson from under the seat. He was examining the loads, noticing it had been fired since he cleaned it and wondering a little about this, when Martha came and laid a hand anxiously on his arm. 'Gibson! What are you doing?'

'Got to do *something*,' he told her quietly. 'Or that pair's going to start thinking I'm afraid of them!'

'Please!' She shook her head, her eyes frightened.

'Martha, I can't back away from 'em! It means too much to us. We didn't come all that distance, and go through what we have, just to let them bluff us out!'

'I'm afraid they won't stop at a bluff!'

He replaced the spent shell, from a box he kept under the seat. He snapped the cylinder back in place. 'I'll go as far as they make me!' He glanced over at Jody and the girl, busy near the fire. Something hard rose in his throat and he swallowed. 'Keep the children here. Whatever you do, don't let Jody try to follow me.'

He read the protest in her face, but she didn't argue. Yaeger squeezed her arm, once. Then abruptly he turned and moved out of the fireglow, into the dense starlit darkness, trying not to remember that he might be turning his back on his family for the last time.

Dry grass crumpled under his heavy shoes. The gun felt strange in his hands. As he walked he stuffed it into the bib of his overalls, only the butt showing. He supposed there was still a hope—but a fading one—that this trouble could be settled without a fight.

The claim jumpers didn't have much in the way of a camp—their horses and gear and a scatter of stuff from a saddle pack. They were seated side by side on a fallen log, with a coffeepot on the fire, and passing a tin cup and a whiskey bottle back and forth between them. They looked up as Yaeger walked into the circle of firelight and stopped.

For a moment no one spoke. Then one of them, with a grin narrowing his eyes, said loudly, 'Well! Decided to back down and get the hell off our claim?'

'You know I ain't,' Gib Yaeger said. 'Since it ain't your claim!'

The two exchanged a look. The bigger of them set down the bottle and got slowly to his feet, hitching his gunbelt. 'Don't be a fool, partner,' the man said reasonably. 'You got no business bucking odds. You're a man with a family to think about.'

'I'm thinking about 'em,' Yaeger said coldly. The claim jumper was walking toward him now, still not touching the gun. The other had got to his feet. Gib Yaeger thought suddenly they were maneuvering to put him between them, but he stood his ground.

'We're willing to give you a chance, partner,' the big one told Yaeger, still in his gentle purring voice, still pacing forward. 'You just pack up your stuff and take your kids and get out of here. Do that, and we won't hurt anybody.'

Gib Yaeger swallowed. 'And if I don't?'

'Why, in that case—' He shrugged and reached for his gun.

But he was too deliberate. He hadn't read the desperation in this man he was baiting; he must not have seen the gun handle thrusting out of the bib of Yaeger's tub-faded blue overalls. A savage need moved Yaeger's arm. He fumbled at the handle of the gun, yanked it out; and then, because he had never shot at a man and this one still hadn't completely cleared his weapon from the holster, Gib

Yaeger used the heavy barrel as a club.

It took the man solidly on the side of the skull. It knocked the hat from his head and dropped him like a rock, face down. The second one only stared helpless and unmoving as Yaeger swung the gun muzzle on around and punched it at him.

'Now, *you* pack up.' He didn't recognize his own voice.

'Sure! Sure, mister!' The man's tongue was suddenly stumbling over itself. 'I ain't armed. He had the only gun. We was just running a bluff on you!'

'Take your gear and get out,' Gib Yaeger ordered wearily. 'You haven't got much time.'

The reaction hit him later, after he'd listened to the two horses moving off into the darkness, the second carrying the man he'd struck, lying face down, across the saddle. When he knew they had gone, he finished stomping out the remains of the fire, making sure no live sparks were left. Only then did the aftermath of fear and strain start him trembling, so that he had to let himself down onto the fallen log until it was past—elbows on knees, head hanging, the Smith & Wesson heavy in his hands.

How long he sat there he didn't know, but he roused with a start as he heard Martha calling his name, fearfully. He answered and rose and went to meet her, taking her into his arms and holding her close in the dark night while she broke briefly into tears. 'It's all right,' he said soothingly, over and over. 'Could have been a lot worse. We're lucky it wasn't!'

She tried to stop crying, apologized when she couldn't. He patted her shoulder, realizing all that was involved in this storm of weeping—the fatigue of the long trek out from Wisconsin, the anxieties of the day just spent, the uncertainties of the future. And, of course, the new life swelling in her.

Yaeger had somehow lost sight of the fact she was so near her time. 'Maybe we'll have the first one born in the Strip,' he said, holding her. 'We got to hurry and make things ready for him . . .'

That served the purpose. She was herself again, and he sent her on back to the camp. 'I'll take one more look around,' he said. 'To make sure everything is good and quiet.'

So much to do, he thought as he stood alone again in the darkness. He was already setting up a timetable. When old Oklahoma was opened, three years ago, they'd held the run in April; it had given people a spring and summer to make their improvements, and turn their ground and at least put in some kaffir and sorghum to harvest for winter. The middle of September certainly seemed a strange time of year for the bureaucrats in the government to hand a man a piece of raw ground and tell him, 'Here! Take this, and go live on it! And see to it you've got a house built and ten acres under cultivation by March . . .'

The run of his thoughts was broken, suddenly, as he heard the brittle grass break underfoot and realized someone was approaching. New alarm brought his hand up, leveling the Smith & Wesson. He let the gun barrel sag, in astonishment, when he saw this was a woman—walking slowly, thrown offstride by the weight of the suitcase she carried. Yaeger fumbled and shoved the gun away.

She stopped and dropped the suitcase into the grass, and straightened.

'Where in the world did you come from?'

'The next claim. I don't want to be any bother—but with night coming on, and no way to make a fire—'

'You're all alone over there?' Yaeger exclaimed.

'I thought my husband would surely be back before this.' She repeated anxiously, 'I wouldn't want to cause you any trouble.'

'With no fire, I bet you haven't eaten anything.'

'I'm afraid not.'

Quickly he moved to her. 'Come right over to the camp. My missus will have some grub ready, shortly. Yaeger's our name. Here, let me have that.'

'We had an accident,' the woman explained. 'Lost our wagon and all our supplies—

everything except what's in there. I was afraid to leave it behind.'

Carrying the heavy suitcase by the rope that held it together, Yaeger took her elbow. 'Watch your step, now,' he said. 'And don't worry any about putting us out. Martha will be happy to meet her new neighbor.'

They walked across the treacherous uneven footing where Yaeger had run his firebreak furrows, and came toward the camp. She looked around at the cheery place, the fire streaming sparks toward the stars, and lantern glow spreading its warm smear of light across the wagon canvas. Yaeger had taken down the overjets, the wagon box extensions to which the hickory bows were fastened; this, as he had planned, would serve as a kind of tent and make do for living quarters until a soddy could be built. Boxes and piles of household belongings stood neatly about where they had been unloaded. Outlined against the campfire was the lyre-shaped back of Martha's favorite rocker.

She and the children gathered quickly to meet their neighbor. Martha, taking one look at the younger woman's tired face, slipped a friendly arm about her waist and said, 'You just make yourself at home! Supper's all ready, such as it is. What did you say your name was?'

'Jean Lavery.'

She was a pretty thing, a bit thin but well-featured according to the fireglow and the lantern. Yaeger said, 'You must be the folks Stormont told Jody about.'

He thought afterward the woman's reaction to the name was strangely quick. 'Oh, you know him? He was very kind to us today. I don't know what we'd ever have done!'

Gib Yaeger nodded thoughtfully. 'He's a strange fellow, that Stormont. I think he's fighting something—most likely, in himself. He wants the world to think he carries a chip on his shoulder; and he doesn't care much for what the likes of us are doing to this country. Yet it doesn't keep him from going out of his way to do a kindness.'

He leaned to toss another cottonwood chunk into the fire. Martha had the Dutch oven out of the fire now and was dishing up pan bread and beans, pouring coffee from the battered and blackened pot. Jody carried their guest's plate to her, where Jean Lavery had, with protests, seated herself in the rocking chair. Yaeger came over, juggling his own tin plate and cup, and took a place on the brass-bound trunk nearby.

'This is delicious!' the girl exclaimed. 'I don't think I've ever been so starved!'

'Your husband, now,' Yaeger asked. 'Where did you say he went?'

'Well, we understood from Mr. Stormont there was a townsite not too far from here, and a land office. Paul set out to get our claim registered, and to see if he could locate some food and supplies to replace what we lost this afternoon. Frankly, I'm a little worried about him.'

'Tell me, is he a country man?'

She hesitated, as though she hated admitting it. 'Well—no. Not exactly.'

'Then, in his place, I doubt if I'd feel much like trying to find my way back, after dark—a strange land like this, no roads, no buildings. I'd say, give him till morning. I'll be heading for this Comanche townsite myself, come daylight. If your man hasn't shown up by then, we'll have a look.'

She said, 'You're very kind.'

'Meanwhile, you spend the night with us. Can't stay on that claim alone.'

At that the girl tried to protest. 'I've imposed on too many people today! That's not what I came to this country for.'

Yaeger silenced her with a shake of his head, as he rose and dropped his empty plate into the wreck pan. 'Let's not argue about it. A person's wrong to think he can stand always by himself. If we're to be neighbors, we might as well start working at it.'

He didn't give her a chance to protest. A proud person, he thought—proud and independent. He could understand, being that kind himself. But that husband of hers . . . Gib Yaeger shook his head, not much liking what he had heard about the man. To leave a woman alone, in this savage country, with darkness coming on, was damned poor sense. It wasn't so far to Comanche townsite, that he couldn't have made it back if he'd put his mind to it.

Something about it filled Yaeger with a nameless premonition.

Bill Ivy had his back against a tree trunk and was gnawing at the meat of a jack rabbit he'd knocked over, when he heard the riders coming in. It sounded like a bunch of them, and they were pounding straight toward his fire, shouting and yelling. He heard one of them bawling out the range and township and section number of his own claim, shouting, *'Clear off! Clear off!'*

Face gone hard, Bill tossed aside the rabbit leg and made a lunge to scatter his fire with the kick of a boot. But at the last moment he turned instead and grabbed up an armload of dry fuel and dumped it onto the blaze; and as the flames leaped up, crackling and popping with an explosion of flying sparks, he turned and ran for the brush and there flung himself belly-flat, slithering around with his belt gun rising in his hand.

The riders swarmed in, seconds afterward. They rode right into camp and pulled up, yelling questions back and forth as their horses milled and they looked in vain for the owner of the fire. Bill thought sourly, Damn fools must be green at this game, to put themselves in the firelight! And, settling on one he judged to be their leader, he dropped his sights on this man and let loose a shot that took the hat right off him and sent it kiting into the darkness.

The man cried out and clapped a hand to his head. Guns gave back the firelight as the near-dozen riders gave startled reactions and jerked around, vainly hunting for Bill. His elbows propped on the ground and the six-shooter steady in both hands, he warned them with a shout: 'The next one ain't gonna be aimed at no hat!'

He thought for a moment they would break and scatter like quail. They did not look like much—a ragtag bunch of riffraff, small-fry border toughs who were not apt to stand up to an enemy they couldn't see or overwhelm by sheer numbers. But one of the lot seemed to think he had located Bill, perhaps by his voice or by the afterimage of that gunshot. He threw down and drove a bullet into the shadows, to clip dead leaves from a bush perhaps two yards from Bill's prone shape.

With no compunction at all, Bill swung his gun on this man and pulled the trigger. Powder-spark streaked from the muzzle; through the flash he saw the rider jerk and start to crumple.

Somebody caught the man before he could leave his saddle. A voice cried: 'Lat! Goddamn it, Lat, he got Jenkins! Got him bad!'

Now there was real confusion. Amidst the milling and yelling, someone in the crowd bawled, 'I think there ain't more than one. Let's clean the bastard out!' Bill didn't scare. He knew, in spite of the odds, this bunch of men had been caught on the defensive and they were not likely to get off it. Instead of hunting cover or trying to scatter the target as they should have done, they were turning to their leader for instructions. And that one sat motionless, still clutching for his missing hat.

To help him, Bill put out a second warning, 'Sure, there's only one of me—but I got plenty of targets, and lots of lead.'

Demonstrating, he fired again, sending his shot so close to the leader's horse that it gave a buck and Lat had to grab the reins with both hands to keep from being thrown. Instantly Bill was scrambling up, fading to one side in the darkness. Another of the horsemen shot wildly and the lead struck the bole of a tree. Bill took cover behind it, leaning out long enough to throw a bullet directly into that clot of men and horses. It stung an animal on the rump and the horse squealed and swung around, striking a second horse and driving it straight through the leaping campfire.

And then, they did scatter. It came without leadership or any plan. Panic just seemed to touch the lot of them and suddenly they blew apart, every man hitting for the nearest escape. Bill stood where he was and thoughtfully thumbed shells out of his belt to replace the ones he'd emptied, and listened to the thunder of the hoofs scatter and fade. Once out of range, he knew of course that they would collect again and then it would be up to the leader, Lat, to rally them and decide the next step.

The Outlet, tonight, would be full of gangs like that one, busy—with guns and force of numbers—cleaning the land of its original stakers and garnering claims for themselves. Well, if they wanted Bill Ivy's there were probably enough of them to take it; but it would cost them.

He replaced the last of the empties and clicked the cylinder into place, after which he faded back a little deeper into the timber. There he halted, his whole body gone quickly tense, for he was certain he had heard hoofbeats strike somewhere to the west. That would mean they were splitting to circle and surround him. It was so definitely the thing he'd have done himself, under the circumstances, that it took a long five minutes of waiting to convince Bill that they had done nothing of the sort, and that what he had heard was nothing more than imagination.

The night grew older; the disk of light spread by his fire began to contract as the fuel burned itself out. And finally Bill had to admit that the danger was ended, and Lat and his men had ridden away and left him his claim without a further contest.

'Yellow bellies!' he grunted contemptuously,

and shoved his gun back into its holster. He knew that type, from long experience. In Bill Ivy's cynical philosophy, they made up a majority of the human race. They banded together to seize what they wanted, but even so a single brave and determined man could stand them off and send them scooting.

His first visit from such as Lat's crew might not be the last, before this night was over. But alone as he was, he knew no moment's doubt that he could keep his claim, and hold it against any number. The man who took this choice quarter section from Bill Ivy was damn' well going to have to show the color of his money, first!

CHAPTER SEVEN

Without fanfare, the sun rose and it was like the opening of an oven door. The sky hung blank, and brassy with a remaining taint of yesterday's long fires. The wind came up out of the south again with more of its punishing intensity. On the seat of the freighter, Stormont's companion ducked his head.

'Another bad one!' the mule skinner grunted. 'What good do the damn' fools think this land is going to do them, now it's theirs? I'm no farmer but I've got sense enough to know a desert when I see one!'

'It wasn't always this way,' Stormont said. 'It's a dry cycle that's shaping up. I've seen the Strip as green and pretty a piece of graze as you ever laid your eyes on.'

'I'll have to take your word for that!' The teamster pointed a thumb that was splayed and calloused by the friction of the broad leathers. 'Would you look yonder?'

In a bone-dry creek bed lined with drooping cottonwoods, a bunch of men and a woman or two were clustered about a slow seep of muddy water, trickling out of what had once been an active spring. There was hardly enough moisture now to blacken the sand, yet these people had armed themselves with every possible container, from buckets to empty cans, and they were quarreling for turns.

The hot wind swept up the arroyo, rattling dead leaves on the trees and flinging gritty dust against the angry faces.

'Thousands of them,' the mule skinner said, 'just like these. How do they expect to live?'

Stormont shrugged. 'The first winter will finish most of them. You'll see them start pulling out, come snow fly.'

'Comanche, just ahead . . .'

Comanche townsite had been planted adjacent to a flag station and water tower on the railroad; it stretched up a sloping rise from the tracks. The place literally swarmed. It had been marked off by government surveyors into some dozen square blocks, and unbelievably this small space had been overrun now by a crowd that Stormont numbered at something like twenty thousand. Already tents and crude shacks were going up on nearly every city lot. The hubbub seemed deafening, topped by the squeal of saws and pounding of hammers.

Raised dust hung over the place. There was not a tree, not a scrap of shade.

'Swing down by the railroad,' Stormont ordered and they pulled wide, following the broad tracks earlier freight rigs had already ground out of prairie sod. Eventually, supplies for Comanche and the hinterland it served would come in directly by rail; but for the time being, and under the present heavy demand, mule freight remained the life line. Already, with teams barely rested, the first wagons to roll in yesterday were heading north for a second load.

Stormont made a mental note that he'd have to check on the building of mule pens, so that fresh stock could be brought down from Caldwell as quickly as possible and keep the wagons moving.

Near the foot of what would be Comanche's main street, stood the railroad's big water tower; riding nearer, they could see the crowd of people thronging underneath it to get at the single tap. Stormont heard someone shouting '. . . got into town all right, but the last three miles I only kept my Goddam hosses alive by feeding 'em whiskey out'n a spoon!' And another answered, 'You was lucky. My old hayburner died betwixt the stirrups! Fell right down under me!' No one seemed to be paying any attention to a man who stood with head bared and arm raised as he shouted at the crowd. The man was preaching, Stormont realized suddenly—Comanche's first sermon.

He had forgotten this was a Sunday . . .

They left the scene behind, and raised thunder from loose planks that had been laid between the tracks to ease the heavy rigs across. Here, beyond the rails, Tom Chapman had set up temporary headquarters.

Crews were laboring to empty a pair of the big wagons, and as fast as the lumber and supplies could be stacked other Chapman clerks were selling it to customers from the townsite. A white-haired man with a green eyeshade, and a ledger book under his arm, yelled at the driver of the new wagon and pointed out where it was to be unloaded. Yonder, Stormont saw the mule pens already completed; there was even feed and water, that Chapman had somehow managed to collect here for his animals.

Now Stormont saw the headquarters tent. He picked up his blanket roll, tucking it under his arm, and setting his boot on a spoke of the big front wheel let its slow turning carry him to the ground. He called back, 'Thanks for the lift,' answering the skinner's wave of arm; when the wagon had rolled past he walked through its settling dust toward the tent.

Tom Chapman himself was there, working at a deal table; he had the haggard, unshaven look of a man who had pushed himself too hard, without rest. In the tent behind him was a rumpled, unmade army cot; hanging from the pole was a lantern with its chimney dark with soot. He looked up and at sight of Stormont his tired face broke in pleasure. He tossed aside his pen and leaned back, nodding. 'I was hoping you'd show up this morning. We've got a lot of things to work out.'

'That's what I'm here for. How's it going?'

'Smooth—barring the usual, expected hitches. The stuff is coming through, and we're handling it.'

'I checked with the railroad in Kansas City last night,' Stormont said. 'They'll keep up their schedules into Caldwell.'

'Good enough,' said Chapman, and laid his big hands upon the paper-littered desk in front of him. His glance moved past Stormont, out into the dust-thick stir of activity, across the tracks toward Comanche. The other man turned, pairing his look.

'So this is it!' Lee Stormont murmured.

'Right across there—close to the railroad siding: That's where the freight yard and office will go up.'

'Looks like a pretty good proposition. "Freight King of the Cherokee Outlet,"' Stormont quoted, looking at him shrewdly.

'It's what they're already starting to call you. Is that what you want, Tom?'

The older man made an impatient gesture. 'I thought you knew me better! I'm past the age for empire building. Anyway, the big days of wagon freighting are done for. The railroads have made an anachronism of us.'

'Over the long hauls, maybe. There's plenty left for wagons and teams to do, places where the tracks don't run yet and never will.'

'You're right. And if I can just carve a little piece of that business for myself—enough to take care of me and Lucy—I'll be satisfied.'

'The day I see you satisfied,' Stormont said, smiling, 'is a day I'm not looking forward to. Because then I'll know age has caught up with you!'

Tom Chapman changed the subject. 'Did you see my girl before you left?'

Stormont nodded. 'Last evening at the hotel. She's doing fine. The Binghams are taking good care of her. But I'm afraid she's apt to get lonesome, up there.'

'It won't be for long,' the other said confidently. 'I've got a building lot already spoken for. She'll be in her own home by Thanksgiving.'

'No sooner than that? Tom, you can't leave her sitting around that Kansas town, all by herself!'

'I don't like that part of it, but you can't rush the kind of house I'm planning for her!

It'll have everything—bow windows and a side porch and a brick chimney and all the gingerbread a woman could ask for! She thinks this is a wild country I've brought her to. Well, she steps inside that house, I'm going to have her thinking she never left Missouri!'

And Lee Stormont thought, You're talking about the house you never got around to building for her mother—the promise you never had time to keep . . . Aloud he said, 'You got any food around here?' He looked into the tent with its sparse furnishings.

Chapman shrugged. 'What's food? I'd forgotten.'

'Well, *I* haven't!' Stormont indicated the pile of paper work that littered the table in front of the other man. 'If you can knock off there long enough, maybe we can go and round up some breakfast.'

'Come back in about a week. Maybe I'll be caught up with myself!' He added seriously, 'I'm not really hungry right now. More important to get this out of the way. You go along.'

'Suit yourself. I'm hungry. I'll see what I can scare up—and have a look at this town.'

He stowed his blanket roll in the tent, folded his coat and left that as well; but he kept his gun and belt. He was rolling up his sleeves as he picked his way through the orderly confusion of the wagon yard, stepping wide to make way for another rig that lurched across the tracks. And thus Stormont set foot for the first time in Comanche.

Near at hand the crush of people was nearly overwhelming. Noise closed about him, suffocating as the heat that poured out of a brassy sky. Everywhere he looked Stormont saw umbrellas raised as shields against the sun, but they didn't do much good; the ground underfoot, beaten into floury dust, seemed to reflect the shimmering light into a man's face like the surface of a mirror.

He saw a squad of soldiers keeping order at the land office but otherwise, with no law except a man's gun and his fists, there was little more than chaos. Men stood in clots where street corners would be, and disputed loudly over the ownership of claims. Others hammered raw yellow lumber into the shape of buildings, or swore as they fought the bulky awkwardness of canvas tents.

Despite the clearly marked survey lines, attempts had been made to stake lots in the middle of the streets themselves. A farm wagon, rattling through with a half-load of lumber, ran into trouble trying to make clearance and as Stormont watched this became a major fight, involving a dozen men. Heads were broken, tents went down. The wagon overturned and its horses squealed in terror. Stormont walked on minding his business.

Toward the heart of the townsite, where the

swarming was thickest, gamblers had set up their portable games—over-and-under, three balls, chuck-a-luck, and dice case. Stormont pushed his way into the crowd before a tent; here food was being served across a crude plank board by a man in a derby and a filthy apron. For his dollar he was served a slab of cold beef between slices of dry bread and a tin cup of unsweetened coffee, and knew he was lucky to get that.

Later he heard a woman's voice call his name; turning, surprised, he saw a familiar-looking wagon rolling slowly through the press of traffic. On the seat were Gib Yaeger and Jean Lavery, and quickly he worked his way over to them. He placed a boot on a wheel hub as Yaeger stopped his team.

'Hello, there,' he said. 'So you met your neighbors. What do you think of this?'

He indicated the new-born town, the boiling activity. The woman looked around and shook her head. 'I can't believe it!'

Stormont found himself watching her closely. Yesterday he had seen her in the aftermath of the overturning of her buckboard, and the escape from the burning gully. Her clothing torn, her skin scratched and blackened by dirt and ashes, she had seemed to him then to hold the promise of beauty. Now he saw that the promise was true. Rested and refreshed, with her fair hair caught up attractively beneath the edge of a poke bonnet, she was as handsome a woman as he had known she would be.

Gib Yaeger, beside her on the wagon's hard seat, shifted the reins and said, 'I've heard of towns springin' up overnight; didn't know it would look like this!'

'I suppose it will begin to shake down in a day or two,' Stormont answered. 'Look more like a town, after about nine-tenths of this mob breaks up and sifts back to where it came from. Until then, I don't think I'd want to try hanging around here too long. Either of you!'

'Sure not our intention,' said Yaeger. 'Got our claims to file; and then, Miz Lavery's a little concerned about her husband. Haven't seen him, have you?'

'No, I haven't.' He added quickly, 'Anything wrong?'

'He tooken off last night, hasn't made it back yet. Of course,' Yaeger added with an obvious aim of reassuring the woman, 'there's no reason to worry. He could be anywhere in this swarm.'

'He left to file on our claim,' Jean explained. 'And to get some supplies if he could find them. I'm afraid he might have got lost.'

'Did he have a gun?'

'No,' Gib Yaeger replied. 'But I keep telling Miz Lavery he's a grown man. I reckon he knows how to take care of himself.'

Remembering Paul Lavery's panicky

behavior yesterday under stress, Lee Stormont wasn't that sure. But he said only, 'I'll keep an eye open.'

Jean thanked him with a smile, and Yaeger picked up the reins, saying, 'Speak of filing claims—I reckon that's what I'd better be doing.'

'The land office is yonder.' Stormont pointed out the unpainted wooden building. A straggling queue extended from its doorway, far beyond the edge of the townsite—scarcely seeming to move. Yaeger shook his head with a sigh.

'More waiting in line!' he grunted. 'I swear, it don't rightly seem the way to build a territory!'

But he was in good humor as he yelled up the horses. The wagon rolled on, making way somehow through the clutter and mill of humanity; and Stormont, frowning, watched until it was out of sight.

Just what about this fellow Lavery?

He hated to bother. You didn't adopt someone, just through the act of lending him a hand in a bad moment—foolish to get in the habit of acting like it, when you had problems of your own. Still, the man had a wife and his wife was concerned for him. And if he hadn't come to harm, overnight, then where was he?

If he was a drinking man, now . . .

The idea lifted Stormont's head, to gaze thoughtfully toward the familiar shape of a big tent that was the largest single structure in Comanche; as he looked, his eyes narrowed. Murray Lenson must have had a crew working all night, to have got his establishment set up and opened for business this morning. Comanche's first and—at the moment—only saloon was doing more business than the land office. A moment's hesitation, and then Stormont decided with a shrug. He might at least check. It would only take a moment.

He dodged through the street traffic and across lots, through dust and wood chips and trash, moving clear as one rough-carpentered side of a building frame was lifted into place by sweating, swearing men. A buckboard with a runaway team came tearing across the townsite, scattering dust and confusion and profanity in its wake. It narrowly missed a corner of Murray Lenson's tent and some of his customers were pulled out to yell it by. Stormont shoved through them and inside.

The roar of drink-loosened voices, the stomp and shuffle of boots on the crude board flooring Lenson had put down, assaulted his ears; it was stifling here, under canvas that filtered the sun's light and concentrated its power. Almost hopeless, trying to single out any one face in the constantly shifting mob around him.

He saw an opening at the bar, one of the two plank bars that ran the length of the tent, and against his better judgment moved in and ordered a drink. It was at least wet, but Lenson's stock hadn't improved since yesterday evening. As he fought to keep from gagging, a man next to him said, 'Terrible stuff.' Stormont nodded, and the other added, 'But if he's thirsty, a man will drink even this.'

Wiping his mouth on the ball of his thumb, Stormont gave the speaker a glance. He shaped up as a tall, spare figure, about even with Stormont's own height but lacking a good fifteen pounds of his weight—and Stormont carried no extra flesh. He was a city man, better dressed than most of these. He said now, 'Looking for someone?'

Stormont, preoccupied, didn't bother to answer.

'Hayes McClure is the name. I wonder if we might do business? I'm in the market.'

This time Stormont gave him a longer attention. 'Market? For what?'

'Investment properties.'

'Buying claims, you mean—before they're proved up? That's not legal, mister.'

The other shrugged. In the filtered glare of sunlight through heavy canvas his face looked sallow, dry-skinned despite the heat. His eyes were dark, the mouth thin-lipped but humorous. He smiled now, and his mouth quirked around the slim cigar that was thrust in a corner of it. 'Nobody is letting it stop him. It wouldn't stop me, if it happens you've got a claim for sale.'

'Suppose I took your money—and then didn't get off?'

'I guarantee,' the other said quietly, 'you'd get off!'

Stormont looked at him a moment longer, and then shook his head. 'I've got no claim—period. If I had, I wouldn't let some fly-by-night speculator get his hands on it!'

Hayes McClure didn't like that. His eyelids drooped slightly; there was a quick stir of muscles, ridging up beneath the man's sallow checks. But Stormont scarcely noticed.

He was looking toward the center of the big tent, where someone at a portable dice table appeared to have a winning streak going. Shouts were rising, building in volume with every roll he made. And now Stormont saw his face—streaming with sweat, the lips pulled back as he shook and let the cubes go bouncing down the alley. Surprisingly enough, the lucky player was Paul Lavery, himself.

The screen of intervening bodies closed again. Quickly putting aside his empty glass, Stormont started elbowing through the crowd.

He heard the point being called by a dozen voices around the table, and pushing his way to the table saw Lavery throwing down bills in front of a sweating house man. The young fellow was drunk, Stormont thought—not so much with Lenson's bad whiskey as with the exhilaration of his own lucky streak. 'Come on, come on!' he was saying loudly, waggling a hand at the stickman. 'You fading me, or not?'

The man hesitated. 'That's a lot of money you've taken already,' he said. 'The house sets a limit.'

He was met by a chorus of jeering. The crowd wanted Lavery to have his play so they could ride with him; the house man, stalling, looked around for help. And then he showed a look of relief, and following his glance Stormont discovered Murray Lenson himself, legs apart and hands in the pockets of his tight-fitting trousers. It was plain that he didn't care for the situation, but Lenson was measuring the temper of the crowd against the safety of his tent and equipment. He made his decision and told his man, 'Go ahead. Fade him.'

As the house man shrugged and dropped greenbacks onto the felt, Stormont continued for some reason to watch Murray Lenson. Thus he caught the look and the nod that passed between him and a big fellow who had unobtrusively worked his way now into the inner fringe of the crowd, across the table from Stormont. This was a man named Lat Roan, that he'd seen a time or two up in Caldwell and heard identified as Lenson's right arm. Seeing the bulk of the man, and the gun and holster at his waist, Stormont could guess now what the term meant.

He felt himself go tense.

If Paul Lavery was in danger, he seemed

totally unaware of it. He was warming the dice with his breath, rolling them between his palms, eyes gleaming in a gambler's fever. The cubes clicked and chuckled as he shook them. Suddenly they did their dancing run and as they rattled off the end board somebody shouted, 'Made it!'

But before the dice had more than come to rest, Lat Roan's big fist suddenly swept across the board and snatched them up. Amid howls of protest, Roan gave them the briefest of inspections. He stared down the table at Lavery. 'These bones are fixed!' he said in a carrying voice. 'He's switched 'em!'

'Who says so?' demanded Lavery, and his face was instantly white with rage.

'I say it! And nobody rings loads in on one of Mr. Lenson's games!'

'But I didn't!' Lavery turned to the crowd. 'I tell you, it's not so!'

Stormont saw Murray Lenson watching; for all his disinclination to get involved, he felt a swelling alarm. This was what made him say to the man who held the dice: 'Maybe you'd better pass those things around, mister. Give the rest of us a chance for a look . . .'

CHAPTER EIGHT

Roan turned, slowly. '*I've* looked at 'em. That's enough.'

'Just the same, I think you'd better pass them!'

Across the table, Lat Roan let his shoulders settle a little, and his head began a curious motion to the right. Cocked on one side, it gave him a slanted stare at his challenger—as though he saw better out of one eye, and favored it. Roan had a big head, even for someone his size. His hair was red and thick and he wore it long, almost burying his ears that lay flat against his skull. A red bush of mustache hung at the end of a huge and predatory nose.

Murray Lenson spoke softly. 'Stormont, keep out of this!'

Lat Roan said, 'He's the same as calling me a liar!'

There was an odd timelessness about the scene, Stormont thought. It could have been the strange half-light filtered by the canvas roof; or perhaps the dead heat trapped within the tent walls worked to make a man lightheaded. He dragged in a long breath of the whiskey fumes, the reek of dirty clothes and sweating men, and he told Lat Roan, 'If you won't let us see those dice, we're all going to *know* you're a liar!'

Then the men in back of Roan yelled and were stumbling and scrambling over one another, as they saw the big, red-furred paw start toward holster. Stormont didn't hesitate. A quick lift of his right boot, and he had set it against the edge of the dice table and it was toppling over against the big man, scattering a flutter of greenbacks onto the rough flooring.

The table wasn't heavy enough to knock him over but it sent Lat Roan backing and broke the rhythm of his draw; Stormont meanwhile had followed through by scooping his own gun out of the holster. He allowed Roan to see the muzzle of it, pointed straight at him; his thumb caught the hammer flange and rocked it back into firing position.

He said, 'Don't pull that gun! Not in a crowd like this!'

Roan left the movement unfinished; he caught his balance and then stood with the overturned table at his feet, his eyes reflecting the storm of anger beating inside him. Keeping him covered, Stormont glanced quickly toward Lenson and saw, moving up beyond him, another man very much of Roan's type—a tough number named Irv Kinoy, also on Lenson's payroll. He quickly let the muzzle of his gun swing over by a little, ready to come to bear on the saloon owner. He said sharply, 'Tell them no, Lenson!'

Lenson eyed the gun. He looked at Roan,

seeing that the redhead wasn't in a position to do anything, and then at the new man who by this time had reached his elbow. He must have known there was no choice. He gave both his men a slight shake of the head, but his scowl was dark.

Stormont began breathing a little easier. Acting while he was still on top of the situation, he stepped over to Paul Lavery who was lost in a fuddled uncertainty. He took the young fellow by an arm and, pointing him toward the entrance, said, 'Let's get out of this!'

The young fellow stirred himself and pulled away, crying, 'My money!' Grimly, Stormont trapped his arm again and this time he got him started toward the entrance. The moment he did so the crowd broke loose with a confusion of shouts and stomping of boots; without having to look back he knew they were falling upon the spilled money, scrambling after it.

He'd planned on that, to take attention away from himself and Lavery. He could hear—Murray Lenson shouting at the mob, helplessly. A moment later they were outside the tent and the scorching wind felt cool after the smothered heat trapped beneath the canvas.

'Damn you!' Paul Lavery jerked free and turned on Stormont, a clenched fist rising. 'Thanks to you, I left my winnings in there on the floor!'

'You got out with your life. They didn't intend letting you keep both!'

The other's lips trembled. They were dry and pale. 'I don't believe it!' he cried hoarsely. 'You don't shoot a man just because he's got a winning streak going.'

'You don't know this country,' Stormont answered. 'Or men like those. Until you do, I'd suggest you stay where it's safe!' He added, 'Why don't you forget it and look for your wife? She's over at the land office.'

'Jean?' The surprise of this seemed to clear part of the anger out of his head. Lavery glanced around, startled. 'In this hell hole?'

'She waited all night for you. She was worried stiff when you didn't get back, and she came looking.'

'I couldn't go back yesterday. It was dark before I could get my claim registered; and I'm not used to traveling at night, in open country.'

'Well, it's daylight now. No reason for you to get lost.'

Lavery favored Stormont with a slow hostile scrutiny. 'You don't think much of me, do you?' he challenged. 'Well, the feeling's mutual. From here on, I'll ask you to stay out of my affairs!'

'From here on,' Stormont answered coldly, 'it will be a real pleasure!'

Gratitude was obviously an unknown word to a man like Paul Lavery; so—one almost felt tempted to say—was simple common sense.

Watching the man's spare figure stride away toward the land office, arms swinging and head held truculently erect, Stormont shrugged. Paul Lavery was none of his business. And neither was his wife.

It was something he was going to have to remember. It would be his mistake if he forgot it, and let himself get involved in something worse than trouble with Murray Lenson.

Just before the dice table went over, Bill Ivy had quit his place at the bar and started forward, thinking his friend Stormont was up against something dangerous—ready to lay gunbarrel across the woolly matting of hair on that red-headed gunman whose back was turned toward him, and help even the odds. Stormont's quick move, and the draw that caught the redhead flat-footed, changed Bill's mind. He hauled up grinning to see his friend handle the situation.

When Murray Lenson was forced to back away and signal his men to hold fire, it didn't much look as though Stormont needed any help. But then the latter turned and started ushering the dice-thrower out of the tent ahead of him, and Bill saw the redhead's stare of pure hatred. He was prepared for the sudden, stabbing move to draw a gun against Stormont's unsuspecting back; he didn't hesitate. He took an impulsive stride forward and his hip struck the redhead glancingly but hard, and with such unexpectedness that it flung the man off balance and sent him to one knee, the gun knocked from his hand.

The man shouted, 'Goddam it!'

Bill plowed right on into the scramble over the spill of money. He spotted one of the greenbacks, but as he leaned down someone in the crowd unknowingly set a boot heel squarely on top of it. Bill, without hesitation, kicked him in the shins. The man howled and danced away and Bill calmly took up the money and inspected it. It was a twenty. He folded it lengthwise, shoved it into his pocket and straightened, to find himself confronted by the angry redhead.

The big fellow had recovered his gun but he seemed to have forgotten it; it hung at arm's length, pointed toward the ground. Head cocked to the right, he gave Bill that odd, slantwise stare of his, out of yellowish eyes that were flaked with red like his hair and mustache.

He said, 'You rammed me, mister.'

Bill Ivy looked him over coolly. He would have walked on past but the redhead checked him with a sideward step, that left them still face to face, their eyes close and almost on a level. The man repeated: 'I said, you rammed me!'

'Did I?'

'You know damn' well you did!'

They stood taking each other's measure like a couple of strange dogs. Murray Lenson must have seen what was going on for he called now, sharply, 'All right, Lat! Forget it!'

Lat! A name and a voice, sounding out of the darkness beyond his campfire last night while he lay searching for targets came back to strike Bill hard. It was no usual name, and a conviction welled coldly inside him that this was the same man who'd led those raiders against his claim and his fire. It must have mounted to his eyes; for Lat Roan's stare altered slightly, the red-flecked eyes narrowing. 'Who you staring at?' he demanded harshly. 'We met before anywhere?'

'Try real hard,' Bill suggested, in a voice edged with steel. 'See if you remember!'

'The voice is familiar . . .' And then Lat Roan *did* remember, and the memory was reflected in the flicker of his eyes and the sudden shallow breath that swelled his chest. Bill Ivy, catching this reaction, was ready for it. He was already starting to bring up his gun from its holster when he stopped, frozen motionless by the sudden compelling pressure of a six-gun barrel rammed against his back ribs.

'No you don't!' said another, warning voice. Bill recognized that one, too. He'd heard it shouting, '*Goddam it, Lat—he got Jenkins!*' But now the speaker was so close he could feel the warmth of his body. 'Let go of the gun,' the man said. Bill complied, and his holster lightened as the weapon was slipped out of it.

The tent was going full blast again, now. The broken table had been cleared away, the scattered money appropriated; Bill and the two Lenson men formed a little island of danger amid the eddies of the heedless crowd. Lenson walked up, scowling. 'What is this, Kinoy?' he demanded. 'I know this man. He's a friend of Stormont's—name of Bill Ivy. What's he up to?'

Kinoy, the man whose gun barrel was still attempting to prize Bill Ivy's rib case, said harshly, 'He's the man we told you about, last night. The one who killed Jenkins.'

Lenson chewed the inside of his lower lip for a moment, studying Bill. Finally he jerked his head toward the canvas partition that masked the rear end of the tent and made a storeroom of it. 'Bring him back here.'

Hayes McClure, at the bar, saw the knot of men moving through the crowd and caught Murray Lenson's summoning motion of the head. He nodded in reply and, after a discreet moment, followed them under the flap in the partition and let it drop behind him. Back here, it was no less noisy but they had privacy of a kind. There were stacks of whiskey barrels and supplies, a cot with a rumpled blanket.

As McClure joined them, Lenson and Kinoy were watching Lat Roan search the prisoner. The redhead's questing fingers had just discovered something in Bill's shirt pocket; he brought out a piece of paper and unfolded it.

It was a registration certificate on a quarter section claim; and as Roan read the numbers his mouth went tight with recognition.

'This is him!' he confirmed, his voice hard. 'We were clearing off a couple likely looking sections last night and we found this boy roosting on one of them. He gave us a bad time. Killed one of our men.'

'I just might do it again!' yelled Bill. 'Give me that!'

He got his hand on the paper and after that the two of them were grappling, clawing, slugging. They stumbled onto the cot and it smashed under them, putting them both on the floor in a tangle of splintered wood and canvas and blankets. Bill took a head blow that jarred halfway down his spine. Roan's knee reached for his groin. Real anger took over then and with an effort he managed to kick free of the blankets that had trapped his spurs and hampered him. He pulled Roan under him and smashed him across the forehead and the bridge of his nose. Blood spurted; Lat Roan yelled in pain.

Then they were rolling, bringing up against a stack of heavy crates that threatened to topple over on them. Lat Roan, on top now, tried with the knee again. Bill blocked it and twisted his head aside, letting a scorching blow of Roan's fist travel past and smash against the floor planks. Roan was pulled off balance. Bill drove a fist upward into that other face, felt blood under his knuckles, and saw the man's red head slammed sideward against the stack of crates. Under the stunning double impact his eyes lost focus and rolled back into his head. Bill, feeling the weight on top of him go momentarily limp, rolled it off and lunged to his feet. At once he was grabbed roughly from behind; he tried to break free, and failed. Panting, he swiveled his head and saw Kinoy holding to one of his arms and Murray Lenson anchoring the other one.

'Are you a complete fool?' the saloon owner demanded.

Before he could answer, Lat Roan was surging up off the floor again, with a roar of fury. His face was a mess, smeared with blood and the nose beginning to swell. He slapped a hand against his holster but the gun had popped out during the fight. Not waiting to look for it, he started again for Bill Ivy.

Hayes McClure said sharply, 'Hold it.'

'Like hell!' Roan struck Bill, full in the face; with a roar the prisoner broke free and would have returned to the battle. But McClure was shouting, 'Damn it! *Stop them!*' And this time Kinoy managed to crook an elbow about Bill Ivy's throat and haul him off, nearly choking him. Murray Lenson had grabbed Roan by an arm.

The fighting ended.

McClure looked at Bill. 'If he'll behave, let him go.' Kinoy released his prisoner and Bill stood rubbing his throat and returning Lat Roan's hostile stare.

'There's no sense in this,' McClure told him flatly. 'We don't have to worry about one claim, more or less. Go ahead.' He indicated the registration paper lying on the floor at their feet. 'Pick it up.'

Bill hesitated, looking around at the others. When no one objected he shrugged and rescued the paper. He saw his hat and got it, too, slapped it against his knee to knock the shape back into it and pulled it on. He touched a knuckle to the side of his jaw and looked for blood but didn't find any.

Hayes McClure, all this time, was observing Bill appraisingly. His humorous mouth tilted around the slim cigar. 'You're a scrapper, aren't you?' He jerked his head toward the big main section of the tent beyond the partition canvas. 'Most of the crowd out there are sheep.'

'I'll dehorn this one!' Lat Roan muttered, glaring his hatred. His eyes were beginning to be lost in the swelling of his battered nose.

Bill said curtly, 'You can try!'

'Shut up!' Lenson told them sharply. 'Both of you! Let Mr. McClure talk.'

Mr. McClure, Bill thought. So *that* was the size of it! He looked at the Easterner with new respect, wondering just what the relationship was. 'So you got a claim registered,' McClure was saying, his attention on Bill Ivy again. 'You don't look like a man who plans to waste five years of his life sweating to prove it up. There's no profit in that.' He puffed a blue cloud of smoke from the cigar. It smelled like an expensive one.

'You have any better suggestions?' Bill asked boldly. 'Like, buying the relinquishment off me?'

'I might. Might have some other ideas, too. What about a drink, while we talk a little?'

Bill grinned. He couldn't resist throwing a look at Lat Roan's scowling, bloody face, to see how the redhead liked this turn of events. All too obviously he didn't.

'I'm your man,' Bill Ivy said.

CHAPTER NINE

For two weeks, now, people had been asking Lee Stormont if in his experience it ever rained here. True, October had at least brought a kind of change. Suddenly the back of the heat was broken; after a day or two of clouds that let down no moisture, the sky cleared again. Autumn rain still failed to appear, but now the sun that shone in a wine-clear blue sky had lost its fierce heat.

Now the winds that scoured the new land came out of the dawn with a sharp knife edge that was a reminder of winter and made a man turn up the collar of his coat. The winds rattled in sun-browned grass, tore the last leaves from the trees that lined the watercourses, and brought from the corners of the sky a high, lonely fluting of wild geese.

Those two weeks had changed the Cherokee Outlet forever.

After a first wild scramble as speculators took their profits and the great mass of losers hastened to clear out, things were finally beginning to shake down into some kind of pattern. Wells and dugouts had been sunk, houses were building, there were even the beginnings of fences and other improvements. Soon, of course, the Outlet would close tight for winter. But on the townsites, a spirit of competition kept things humming.

As long as lumber and nails could be hauled in, hammers would keep up their tattoo and saws would screech and whine. There seemed to be a feeling that the town that moved ahead of its rivals at this initial stage would somehow outstrip them in the long pull. Civic pride waxed hot, where days before had been only restless wind, unbroken sod, and perhaps a prairie dog village . . .

Lee Stormont rode into Pond Creek with the dusty wind at his heels. Lacking the initial impetus of a land office, this seemed destined to be a less important town than Comanche; but it was on the railroad, close to the Kansas border, and so Tom Chapman was opening a branch office to receive freight for the northern sector of the Strip. After two weeks, except for the fact that every building Stormont saw was made of raw yellow boards oozing pine scent and resin, it looked like a town. He dismounted in front of the Chapman office and went inside. His face was grim.

The local agent, a bald-headed man named Tapp, was fitting a window into a hole cut for it in the rough board wall. 'Where is he?' Stormont asked. The other, sweating over his carpentry, nodded toward a door and Stormont passed on through.

Back here were living quarters. Coffee brewed on a small wood stove and filled the room with its pleasant aroma. Stormont got a tin cup off a shelf, poured himself a shot, and took a chair at a wooden table where a man sat hunched with a half-empty cup in front of him. The man's face was gray and he grimaced as he moved, favoring a bandaged right arm.

Stormont, spooning sugar into his cup from a tin can, said, 'How's the arm?'

'Looks like I'll keep it,' the man said. 'Way the damn' thing hurts, I don't particularly care!'

'Tell me what happened.'

'You saw the wagon?'

Stormont nodded over the rim of his cup. 'What was left of it.'

'Then there ain't a lot to tell. They jumped me before I knew what was happening. I tried to get a gun, but they were too much.' He indicated the gunshot arm. 'I swear I tried!'

'That's all right. You were hired to skin mules, not get yourself killed. Neither Chapman nor I ask that.'

Mart Cable had been on the defensive, up to now. Stormont's words seemed to reassure him and he relaxed his uneasy tension. He was a slim young fellow, earnest about his job, looking a little wild just now with a stubble of beard and the pain of his hurt arm.

'Well,' he said, 'after that they cut loose the teams and set me walking, and started to loot the wagon. Afterward, when I looked back, I could see smoke rising above the trees and I knew they were burning it. Couldn't do a thing to stop them.'

The coffee was too hot. Waiting for it to cool, Stormont took out tobacco and made a cigarette. He saw the hurt man looking at it hungrily so he reached over and put it between the other's lips, and popped a match to light it for him. Then, as Cable sat back dragging deeply at the smoke, he started on another. He asked, 'How many were there?'

'I counted half a dozen.'

'Know any of them?'

The slightest of hesitations. 'Hell! The Strip's running wild with outlaws, these days. And they had their faces covered.'

'You could still have spotted something. A voice, or the size of one of them. Something that might be a clue.' He peered sharply at the man, then deliberately tongued the edge of the cigarette he had rolled for himself and twisted the ends. Fishing for a match, he watched Cable's eyes veer and turn from his own. 'You're holding back!'

'Look!' The man was suddenly close to pleading. 'You been pretty decent to work for, Stormont. But I got a wife and kids to think about. I can't stick my neck out!'

Stormont nodded patiently. 'I understand.' He lighted the cigarette, and then had another try at the coffee. He had drained the cup before the other spoke, with great reluctance.

'If it's any use to you, one of 'em—the leader—he was a pretty big fellow. He had on a mask, like the rest, and he kept his hat pulled low. But I could see the edges of his hair. It was red.'

Stormont looked at him quickly. 'A big redhead,' he murmured. 'Lat Roan . . .'

'I never said it!' Cable protested swiftly. 'And don't say I did, because I'll deny it! Why, even if it wasn't him, he'd hunt me out and kill me! That's the kind he is!'

'I said I understood!' But a restless surge of excitement pulled Stormont to his feet, dropping the butt of the cigarette into the dregs of his coffee cup. 'I promised I wouldn't get you in trouble,' he said. 'Meanwhile, if money's bothering you, you stay on the payroll while that arm heals. We need you.'

'Thanks.' Cable looked a trifle shamed. He sat working at his cigarette as Stormont went out.

Quitting the office after a few routine questions to Topp the agent, Stormont returned to his mount, his mind busy with speculation. He took time to examine a shoe he had thought might be coming loose, deciding otherwise. He mounted, then, and rode on up the busy street, so preoccupied he didn't at once recognize the man who stood in the doorway of a building across the way and a hundred yards nearer the shining railroad tracks. He looked up only when Hayes McClure called out his name, in a pleasant greeting; and then he checked his horse, and rode over.

The man stood leaning comfortably against a doorpost, his hands in his pockets. He had taken to wearing boots instead of a city man's shoes, and his face was browning up somewhat under constant exposure to prairie sun and wind. But the cigar in his mouth could have been the same one he was smoking the first time Stormont saw him.

A freshly painted sign on the false front above his head identified the headquarters of McCLURE FREIGHT.

'So this is your outfit,' Stormont said, looking at the sign.

'It's small,' Hayes McClure admitted. 'But it's growing.'

'Pretty damned fast!' He added dryly, 'I thought you were only interested in land investments.'

The other shrugged. 'Anything that will show a profit. I hope you and Tom Chapman aren't afraid of a little competition!'

'Afraid? We welcome it.'

'I understood Chapman was after a monopoly.'

'You understood wrong!'

McClure took the cigar from his mouth and examined the glowing end. 'You just lost another wagon, I hear.'

'That's right. Know anything about it?'

'Just what I hear. What else would I know?'

'That's what I'm asking.'

The man's head lifted, his stare settled on Stormont. It held cold dislike. 'I don't think I care for your questions,' he said sharply. 'You wouldn't be accusing me of something?'

Stormont was in no mood to pull his punches. 'I just know I haven't heard of you losing any wagons.'

'And you're not likely to! Compared to Chapman, I'm not big enough for them to bother with.'

'You're getting bigger. You've grabbed off business that was supposed to have gone to us. Every account Tom Chapman loses because of these raids—you seem to be right there to pick it up!'

'Can't blame me for that,' the other said

bluntly. 'I'm getting a reputation for making safe deliveries. It's my main asset, in trying to compete with anyone as big as Chapman.'

'The customers figure your wagons will be passed up for ours.' Stormont nodded. 'I know. Some of 'em have been frank enough to admit it.'

McClure spread his hands. 'Then why talk tough to me?'

'Because I don't trust you, McClure!' Stormont picked up the reins. 'You told me once, yourself, that you aren't particular about your methods. And you're the one that's mainly benefitting from this trouble we been having. That's reason enough to keep my eye on you!'

The man's eyes seemed to flicker behind their lids. A vagrant trace of anger moved across his cheeks and tightened them. 'I'll tell you now,' he said crisply, 'that's a bad guess!'

'It better be!' Stormont answered, and rode on leaving Hayes McClure standing there beneath his sign. The cold eyes followed him.

When Stormont was gone from sight, a sudden spasm of rage constricted Hayes McClure's tight mouth. He plucked the half-smoked cigar from his lips, and flung it hard into the dust.

* * *

Working by lamplight, Elias Rigby was setting

up the first page of his newspaper. He locked the type in the form, went over it with mallet and block, and the familiar, pungent odor of printer's ink rose as he wielded the roller with deft and practiced strokes. Afterward, ready now, he wiped his hands across the front of his leather apron and reached for a sheet of newsprint.

There was, for Rigby, an emotional quality in this moment, as there had been in every town across the Midwest where he'd set up his hand press and his shirttail full of type. Somehow through the years he'd retained the native optimism that kept a tramp newspaperman going. Even now, when time had thinned the hair on his freckled scalp and dimmed his eyes behind steel-rimmed bifocals, his hands were unsteadied with excitement as he pulled proof on the first issue of the Comanche *Intelligencer.*

Ink smeared his fingers as he glanced over the front page editorial. The phrases, used so often before that they were like well-worn coins, rang true and fresh in his ear as though they had been minted yesterday: 'A new country . . . the last frontier . . . opportunity . . . potential for growth . . .'

A gunshot broke the stillness of the print shop; a second one, and then two more in quick succession. They took him quickly to the door of the small frame building, the proof sheet still in his hands. The shooting, he judged, had been at Lenson's; he shook his head, frowning. Places like that were the canker that ate at the life of a town.

As he stood looking over Comanche town, tallying the changes that could be seen taking place in front of his eyes—the big frame hotel that that man Bingham had just finished, the smaller buildings which were replacing the tents and temporary shacks of Comanche's first hasty settlement—an editorial began to take shape in his mind: about the importance of the coming election of the town's first council, the need of appointing a constable with power to see that law was made effective, before present chaos became a habit.

He watched a horseman ride tiredly down the length of the street, through the slanting ruby light of sunset. Elias Rigby recognized him—Lee Stormont, who worked for big Tom Chapman. Someone like that, he felt, could take hold and keep things in order here. Too bad he was fully occupied with the freighting job. Besides, he struck Rigby as a cynical man, totally indifferent to the ultimate destiny of this town; his attitude repelled the newspaperman as much as his efficiency raised admiration.

No, not Stormont, he admitted to himself, watching the rider turn the corner toward Lenson's. But perhaps someone as like him as possible. He must be found; the hopes of Comanche rested on it . . .

*　　　*　　　*

Lee Stormont heard the shots and knew they had come from the big, raw-lumber barn with which Murray Lenson had replaced his saloon tent; but he didn't let the knowledge deflect his purpose. Turning a corner, seeing the light pouring out of its windows into the red sunset glow that filled the town, he rode straight on and dismounted. Tying, he went deliberately up the steps and in through the glass double doors.

The saloon was as big as the tent had been, with a mahogany bar freighted in from Kansas City, huge wagon-wheel chandeliers, and a wide stairway leading to a balcony on the second-floor level. It was less crowded than the tent, because the excess population of those first days in the Strip had mostly drained away now. The bulk of what was left to frequent a place like Lenson's was the anomalous breed of those who hung around because they had nowhere in particular to go.

Stormont halted just inside the door, his canvas jacket unbuttoned and flung open. The scene before him could have been staged for theatrical effect. The crowd at the bar and gambling tables held motionless, watching a man who lay writhing on the floor near one of the faro tables. A chair had been overturned, a drift of blue gunsmoke tanged the still air.

Now, as Stormont looked on, the one who had tallied straightened, slowly, still holding his smoking gun. It was Lenson's man, Irv Kinoy. He moved forward, took the hurt man by a shoulder and dumped him over onto his back. A gun spilled out of lax fingers, clattered on the floor.

The victim might have been a homesteader from one of the quarter-sections out on the prairie. No one offered to help him. Kinoy, shoving his gun into holster, said loudly, 'He asked for it! Anybody claims the games here are crooked, better be able to back it up!'

He was an oddly built man, with massive shoulders that made him appear almost deformed. As he looked challengingly around him the crowd avoided his stare, turning again to their drinks and their interrupted games.

And then Kinoy was whirling toward the door, as Stormont's boot heels struck the floorboards. The gunman's eyes narrowed. 'You buying into this, Stormont?' he demanded.

His face slowly colored. Stormont didn't even seem to have heard. He was moving past Kinoy, as though unnoticing, and straight toward Murray Lenson's private office where two men stood watching in the doorway.

One of these was Lenson himself; the other, a rather vague sort of person with chest-long whiskers and a drifting eye. Ira Forrester had opened a livery stable in Comanche but it was widely suspected he owed most of his capital to Murray Lenson.

Like the saloon owner, he was running for one of the five seats on the city council. Stormont paid him no more attention than he had the gunman, Kinoy. He told Lenson, 'I'm looking for Roan.'

He met a cold, pale-eyed stare. 'Well? Do you see him?'

'If I did, would I be asking?' The hostility between these two had been an undeclared war ever since the incident of the wrecked dice table, the day after the run. Stormont caught the other's glance moving past him toward Irv Kinoy and he shook his head in warning. 'Don't call anybody over. My business is with Lat Roan.'

The other hesitated a brief second, then said gruffly, 'I don't think Lat's in town.'

'Where, then?'

'Hell, I don't keep tabs on him! He comes and goes. He's his own man.'

'Is he?' Stormont snapped.

Forrester was looking from one to the other, as though vaguely alarmed at what he was witnessing. From the tail of his eye, Stormont saw a couple of men carrying out the one Kinoy had shot; Comanche boasted no licensed doctor as yet, and he only hoped the man's friends would be able to do something for him.

He said, still holding Lenson with his eyes,

'Maybe then you can tell me where he was yesterday . . .'

'You still talking about Lat Roan?' Lenson sounded bored with the subject. 'Well, I suppose he was here around the saloon most of the day.'

'Sure of that? He wouldn't have been over toward Pond Creek, maybe?'

The pale eyes flickered. 'He was here!'

'In other words, you intend to alibi him.' Stormont shook his head in anger.

Murray Lenson became indignant. 'It's plain you're trying to pin something on him. You and Chapman, both, think this town belongs to you—and anybody you don't like can either walk small or get out. Well, we may see about that, after election!'

'Who brought politics into this?' Stormont asked. 'I came here looking for a man. I'm still looking for him. Far as I'm concerned, any alibi you give him doesn't count for a damn!'

The man next to Lenson stirred uncomfortably and clawed at his wispy straggle of beard. 'You shouldn't talk to Mr. Lenson that way,' Ira Forrester protested. 'He's a responsible citizen of Comanche.'

Stormont turned his regard briefly on the livery owner. 'In that case, maybe I'll start holding him responsible for Lat Roan!' The scene was getting nowhere, and leaving a decidedly sour taste in his mouth. There was nothing to do but end it. He did so abruptly, turning on his heel and walking out of there, leaving the two of them staring after him.

In the cool night, he took a long pull at fresher air. Afterward he turned back to his horse, mounted, and rode down the hill toward the railroad tracks and Tom Chapman's fenced wagon yard and freight office, at the foot of Main Street.

CHAPTER TEN

Stormont found two men closeted with Tom Chapman, at his desk in the new headquarters that was redolent of the raw pine lumber it was built from. Big, blackheaded Pete Quilter, down from Caldwell to check some routine matter with his boss, greeted Stormont with a handclasp that left his arm numb to the elbow. The second visitor was a well-built man of about forty, with a direct blue stare and an air of competence. Tom Chapman said, 'You've met Bill Tilghman, ain't you?'

'Sure,' said Stormont, as they shook hands. 'When he was marshal at Dodge.'

Stormont pushed back his hat and leaned his hip against the edge of the door. Out in the main office, a space heater put forth a glow to combat the chill of this October evening.

Chapman said, 'Bill's a deputy federal marshal here in the Territory, now. He happened to drop in and we've been discussing the election.'

'These town elections are tremendously important,' Tilghman said. 'The federal office is understaffed. Until you people put together some kind of local authority, there can't be real law today in the Strip.'

'We've got no law in Comanche, for certain!' Tom Chapman agreed dryly. 'As for order, it's a matter of what a man can carry in his own holster. So far we've been pretty lucky —no real explosions. The riffraff hangs out at Murray Lenson's for the most part, and he's got a crew of guns to keep them quiet. But the sluggings and the shootings still go on.'

'Murray Lenson!' Tilghman repeated, and made a face. 'That two-bit whiskey runner?'

'Don't underestimate him,' Stormont said. 'Lenson's come up in the world, these days. He's somebody to be reckoned with.'

'It's hard to credit!'

'But it's a fact,' Tom Chapman confirmed. 'He has key men listed for every post on the city council. He'll take over if he can, and he'll run this town wide open. I'm worried right now about Election Day.'

'I'll see what can be done about getting some troops up here Tuesday. Governor Renfrow's got enough at stake, I think he could be persuaded.'

'A good idea,' Chapman agreed. 'The town would rest a damn' sight easier.'

'It's not only the towns that are needing law and order,' Lee Stormont said, looking at his boss. 'You just lost yourself another wagon.'

Tom Chapman had been in the act of digging out the bowl of a pipe with a knife blade. Now, slowly, he let both hands drop to the desk tip; his silvery mane gleaming in the lamplight as his big head lifted to stare at Stormont. 'When was this?' he demanded heavily.

'Yesterday. The usual pattern—they looted and burned it, and killed the mules. Mart Cable was driving; they shot him, too, but he'll recover.'

'Thank God for that!'

Big Pete Quitter scowled blackly, drumming the desk with yellow-nailed fingers. 'This is a hell of a note! A dozen outfits lost, in the two weeks since the run! Tom, you're spread too thin to take such losses!'

'Any idea who does these things?' Bill Tilghman demanded. 'Any clue the marshal's office can work on?'

Stormont hesitated. But after all, he had made a promise to Mart Cable; and the identification of Lat Roan was far from certain. He shook his head. 'Afraid not,' he answered, and was aware of Tom's blue eyes studying him thoughtfully.

'Well, there's plenty of freebooters in the Strip,' Tilghman submitted, 'on the make for anything. Men that got shaken out of the run.'

Tom Chapman said, 'From the pattern the raids have taken, I'd say it's more like an organized gang.'

Tilghman frowned. 'Bill Doolin's bunch is on the loose,' he admitted. 'But waylaying freight shipments don't hardly sound like Doolin's style . . .'

'Why the hell do they have to torch the wagons?' Pete Quilter blurted angrily. 'It's a damn' waste! They slaughter the teams—take what supplies they want, and burn everything else!'

'Maybe somebody in the outfit enjoys watching the sparks fly. I've heard of such.'

'A firebug, you mean? And somebody else that likes to shoot mules?' Quilter shook his head. 'I don't believe it! My guess is, they're out to bust us!'

'If it's some competitor, you'd think he'd be able to use the animals and the rolling stock in his own business.'

'Might be too risky,' Lee Stormont suggested. 'Too easy to trace them.'

The marshal's lips pursed thoughtfully, under his full mustache. He asked, 'What precautions are you taking?'

'All my drivers carry guns,' Tom Chapman said. 'But I won't have them risking their lives, just to protect my property. And, as Pete says, I'm spread thin. I've got too many wagons on the road to hire guards for all of them.'

'Where the hell's the Army?' Pete Quilter

demanded. 'And the governor, whatever his name is? Don't they know these supplies are the lifeblood of the Strip—at least till it's able to start producing something of its own? They should be givin' us escorts!'

'Tom just answered your question,' Tilghman told him. 'There wouldn't be enough troops in the whole Territory!'

As Quilter glowered at the desk top, thinking this over, Chapman turned to Stormont. 'What do you think, Lee?'

Stormont dragged a long breath. He scraped the back of one hand across a beard-stubbled cheek, and shook his head. 'Right now I'm too tired to think,' he said. 'But I certainly don't know the solution!' He straightened. 'If nobody objects, I think I'll turn in. I'm not adding a hell of a lot to this discussion.'

'Maybe you'd better,' Tom agreed. 'I'm afraid I'll have to send you over to Woods County tomorrow. There's new business shaping up over that way that needs your personal attention.'

'All right.' A further brief exchange, and Stormont said good night and left the office. It was full dark now, though early still. He stood looking up the hill at Comanche, aglow under the sweep of stars, and hearing its raucous voice. The door he had closed opened again, quietly, and Tom Chapman joined him.

'No change in the weather,' Stormont

predicted.

'Don't look like it.' They stood in silence for a moment. Then the older man said, 'Lee, I know you pretty well. You were holding something back, just now.'

Stormont hesitated. 'I may have some ideas,' he admitted finally. 'But they're nothing to act on. Not yet.'

'Or, to talk about?'

'Sorry, Tom. I gave a promise. But when I get anything definite—you'll hear.'

'That's good enough for me. Just be careful.' Another silence. 'I don't like to admit it, Lee, but for the first time I'm a little scared. I keep thinking of something we said, once—something about getting old. Maybe that's why it worries me, for the first time in my life, that I may have stretched things too far.

'Pete's right, you know. Spread out this way, if somebody's got in mind to break me—they just might have found a way to do it!'

'Any ideas who that somebody might be?' Stormont asked carefully, trying to make out his friend's face in the starglow. He saw Tom shake his shaggy head.

'I'm a long way from being the only freighter in the Outlet. And no doubt some of my competitors can be pretty tough when they want to be. There's that one, McClure, grabbing up business faster than I lose it. But any opinion I had would be sheer guesswork.'

For just a moment, Stormont was tempted

to unburden himself. But until he knew more, he didn't think it was wise to get Tom worked up. A possible identification of Lat Roan, and some ambiguous remarks from Hayes McClure, didn't add up to much. Roan was Murray Lenson's man, not McClure's—not so far as he had any reason to believe; there had to be a better connection than the mere fact he'd first met McClure drinking in Lenson's saloon tent.

So all he said was, 'You're right Tom. Only thing we can do is keep our eyes open, and work it out as we go.'

His trail-worn horse had already been turned over to a stable hand, to be cooled out and fed. He went along the wind-scoured street, now, looking for something to eat, after which he would return to the freight yard and find a place to bed down; if his stomach had been less empty, tiredness would have tempted him to go without the meal.

He tallied the changes here, even in the few days he'd been away. There were new businesses along the lamp-splashed street. Another saloon had opened, that they didn't need; but there were better things too. He saw a freight wagon backed up before a newly completed furniture store, and men unloading stock by lantern light. He passed a drugstore he didn't remember, a barber shop doing business, a dressmaker's place with headless dummies in the window.

When he came abreast with the new hotel and saw it blazing with light, he thought a moment of stepping in to see if his friends the Binghams had arrived yet from Caldwell. He decided against this and was passing on when he heard his name spoken. In utter surprise he turned as Lucy Chapman came out of the doorway and down the steps toward him, into the spill of yellow light from one of the lobby windows.

'Lucy!' he cried. 'What in the world are you doing here?'

'Watching for you.' She smiled directly up at him. Her head was bare but she wore a wrapper over her dress, pulled about her against the chill. He could see the pleasure in her face, the shine of welcome in her eyes. 'I saw you ride in and I thought you'd at least be stopping to say hello. But, you'd have gone right by!'

'Your father didn't tell me you were in Comanche.'

'I came down yesterday, with the Binghams,' she explained. 'Maybe you knew they sold out their place in Caldwell?'

'I knew.'

Something in his manner warmed her. She tilted her head a little, peering up at him. 'You aren't pleased to see me.'

'Not particularly,' he admitted shortly. 'Comanche's a rough place. But I suppose, at that, it's no worse than being left all by yourself in Caldwell.'

'Well,' she said flatly, 'whether you like it or not, I'm pleased to see *you*!'

He frowned, and put a hand to his beard-shagged jaw. 'I don't look like much, right now!'

'Why should I care about that? I know the job you're doing . . .'

A knot of horsemen came along the street at an easy lope, raising pungent dust for the wind to carry and spread out ahead of them in a stinging, gritty fan. As Stormont looked up the lead riders pulled in, and the dust curtain fell away. He stiffened, seeing the big shape and shaggy red thatch of Lat Roan—and the way the man sat staring down at him. Quick caution made him straighten, moving a step away from the girl while one hand made a careless gesture that swept back the flap of his windbreaker and freed his gun and holster.

Before anyone could speak, another rider in the group pushed his mount forward, ranging himself alongside Lat Roan. As this man cuffed back his hat, a kind of sick disbelief shocked through Stormont.

He was looking at the grinning face of Bill Ivy.

'Well!' said Bill, when no one else spoke to break the silence. He hooked a thumb in his belt, that gleamed with lamplight striking off brass-filled loops, and eyed the girl with Stormont. 'If he ain't gentleman enough to give names, guess I'll have to. Bill Ivy's mine.'

Her response was immediate. 'Oh! I've heard all about you! He's told me—you're his best friend . . .'

The grin broadened. 'Guess that's about right.'

Stormont stirred himself. He couldn't keep the anger from his voice. 'Looks to me he's got some new friends!'

'I'll introduce 'em,' said Bill.

'Don't!' The single syllable stiffened Lat Roan, jerking him erect in the saddle. 'Miss Chapman doesn't need to know them!'

As the redhead glowered, Bill cocked an eyebrow at Lucy. 'Chapman's girl, huh? Well, I'm real pleased, ma'am!'

'Since when you been running with this crowd?' Stormont demanded.

'Why, there's nothing wrong with boys like Lat Roan,' Bill said mildly, 'once you get to know 'em.'

'Yeah?' Stormont was uncompromising as he turned to their leader. 'I'll ask you what I asked your friend Lenson: Where were you yesterday?'

The redhead's eyes narrowed. He answered carefully, 'That might be hard to say. We get around.'

'Over near Pond Creek, maybe?'

'No!' The denial came too quickly. 'Nowhere near there!' But before Stormont could catch him up on it, Bill Ivy effectually took the wind out of his friend's sails.

'That's a fact, boy. I was with 'em.'

'*You*?' Stormont could only look at him, wishing that somehow he could have heard wrong. Finally he took a long breath. He shook his head. 'I'm sorry to know that!'

During all this, Lat Roan's head had been swiveling slowly, the way it had of doing when he was getting in a dangerous mood; now he was staring sideways at Stormont, out of the corner of that sharp right eye. He said crisply, 'I don't know what the hell you're hinting at, mister!'

'I don't reckon you'd want me to spell it out!'

'Hey, now!' Bill shifted position and laughed a little, nervously, as he looked from one to the other. 'Let up, boy!' he told Stormont. 'What do you say we call this quits, and have us a drink?'

'With them? At Lenson's, maybe?' Stormont shook his head. 'No, thanks! You know their breed. If it's your taste, Bill, go ahead—and I'm disappointed. But, don't count me in!'

Bill Ivy's manner changed at that. His look grew hard, his mouth lengthened and firmed. He glanced aside at Lat Roan, then nodded to Stormont. 'All right,' he said. 'I won't!'

With a yank at the reins he spurred his mount, and galloped on along the street toward Lenson's. The others remained, ranged behind Lat Roan who considered Stormont for a long moment, as though he had something more to say. But then he looked at the girl, and he gave a loose shrug. As though at a signal the whole group of men spurred away in a sudden burst of hoof thunder.

Lucy turned to Stormont. Her eyes were wide, a dark stain against her face. 'I—don't quite understand . . . You were accusing them of something!'

'Nothing I can prove.'

'And even your friend? Even Bill Ivy?'

'Forget it!' He straightened his shoulders, trying to settle the sick disappointment that was still in him. 'Look,' he said. 'How'd you like to take a ride, in the morning? I've got some friends, out on a claim—some people I think you'd like; I know the Yaegers would like you. I could take you out there, on my way to Woods County. You'd spend the day, and let them bring you back before evening. It would be a change for you. What do you say?'

'Why, I'd love it!' she said. 'If you say they're nice, I'm sure they are.'

'They're the best! We'll have to get an early start, though. I've got distance to cover tomorrow.'

'I'll be ready,' she promised, and a moment later was watching him swing on along the street in his long stride.

Lucy was plainly delighted with the Yaegers, and they with her; Stormont, for his part, was astonished with the amount these people had been able to accomplish on their claim in a little more than two weeks. Gib Yaeger must have been working twenty-four hours a day, for he had his well flowing, his house built, and was already starting to break ground to receive his crops. And he must have done it all alone, except for what help Jody could give him; because, even to Stormont's unknowing and rather embarrassed eye, it was apparent that Martha Yaeger was close to her time—too close to have shared in any heavy labor.

She looked a proud and thoroughly happy woman as she led them inside. It was a single room, walled with sod and roofed with thatch, the inside walls smoothed off with the spade and plastered with gyp from a nearby gully. The floor had been packed with clay. There was a door and a window of actual glass, set in cottonwood frames. Crude as it was, it was Martha Yaeger's first real home. All her possessions, that had been treasured and painfully wagon-hauled half-across the face of a continent, were now set about in permanent position. She showed them to Lucy, while her little girl stood eagerly and politely by—the table and chest of drawers that had been her mother's, the set of hand-painted dishes someone had given her on her wedding day and which had survived, intact, a dozen years of moving in the old wagon. Lucy admired everything, with a warm sincerity that made

Stormont proud of her; he knew very well she had never expected to be a guest in a house made out of dirt and grass.

Afterward, Jody escorted them across the sear brown field to the Laverys' claim adjoining, where Gib Yaeger was helping his neighbors with the construction of their own house. It stood roofless, the walls half raised; Yaeger straightened from cutting sod with a spadebit, while Jean Lavery and her husband paused in their work to watch the visitors come up. As Stormont and Lucy dismounted from their horses, Stormont made the introductions.

Laying sod was a hot and dirty job, even in the mild October sunshine, and Stormont was aware of the contrast the two girls made—Lucy in the riding dress and pert plumed hat she'd brought from Missouri, Jean Lavery with arms bared to the elbows and the dust lying thick in the folds of her skirt. She had pushed her hair up under the brim of an old hat that might have been her husband's, and there was a smear of dirt across one cheek; there was something about her, as she greeted the younger girl without self-consciousness, that made Lucy seem very young indeed.

Paul, who had turned away disgruntled from his labor, underwent a complete change at sight of a pretty face—showed a quick charm and a flashing smile, that seemed out of place on a homestead claim in the middle of the Cherokee Strip. Stormont saw with strong distaste the way he tried to take over the visitor; in sudden intuition, he realized that this smiling, handsome fellow he saw before him now—in the surly, spoiled young man he knew as Paul Lavery—must have been the one that first attracted Jean and charmed her into marrying him. He felt a certain resentment, even while telling himself it wasn't for him to be concerned.

Lucy proved interested in everything she saw; Gib Yaeger demonstrated how the sod was cut with the plow to an even thickness, then chopped out with a spade. He showed her how they laid the courses, grass-side down, and pointed out the two straight crotch posts imbedded in the walls to hold the ridge log. 'You don't want too big a pitch to your roof,' he explained, 'because a rain—if we ever get one!—will wash off the sod you use to anchor the thatch.

'Actually it's better if the bricks can be cut wet—the grass roots hold the moisture and your walls will dry even, without the risk of sagging. Built proper, though, you can figure on a soddy to keep you warm, even in the worst winter a country like this can throw at you!'

'How did you ever learn all these things?' she asked, marveling. He could only answer with a grin and a shrug. But afterward, alone with Stormont, he shook his head and glanced over at Paul Lavery and the two girls. 'I just don't know, Mr. Stormont,' he said. 'About that fellow, I mean. Hate to be that wife of his! She's a fine girl, but *him*—I don't see how he hopes to make it!'

Stalling, Stormont asked: 'How are your affairs going?'

'Oh, we're gonna be all right. Now we got the house built, we'll stick out the winter. Lots of folks are planning to pull out of the Strip, go back to Kansas or old Oklahoma and wait till spring. But the Laverys'—and he reverted to the topic that was troubling him—'they got no place to go. And that fellow's not ready to last a winter out here! Honest, I'm worried!

'I was wondering, any chance he might find work of some sort in Comanche? From what his wife says, he's done a lot of town jobs—bookkeeping and so on. He wants to he his own boss, but I bet if he was offered a spot in some nice warm office or store for the winter, he'd jump at it!'

Stormont frowned. 'Tom Chapman could use another clerk,' he said thoughtfully. 'If he doesn't think so, I imagine I could persuade him.'

'Hope you will,' Yaeger said. 'Take a load off my mind. I got enough of my own affairs to think about, with winter coming fast and Martha due about any time now . . .'

They left it at that. Stormont had distance to cover and within the hour he was riding on, having Yaeger's assurance he'd be glad to see that Lucy Chapman got back to town safely, later in the day. From a little distance he turned in saddle to look back at the work on the unfinished house. He saw Jean Lavery bend for a heavy strip of sod and carry it to lay it in place, and his shoulder muscles ached in sympathy; it was back-breaking work for a man, let alone a woman. His resentment against Paul Lavery deepened, and then he shrugged and turned away.

When was he going to remember that their affairs were none of his? Better if he were never to see either of them again. But, as he rode across the autumn-browned prairie, past the homesteads in their various stages of completion, the two images of Jean Lavery and Lucy Chapman traveled in his brooding thoughts.

CHAPTER ELEVEN

The ballot box, that was supposed to transform Comanche from a clutter of raw-board buildings into an organized community, had been set up in the land office; and there was a detail of soldiers from Fort Sill to help keep order at the polls. Up to now the voting was turning out quiet and orderly enough, despite the tensions involved in determining who, in a town less than a month old, was a qualified resident.

Tom Chapman and George Bingham had cast their ballots early, as befitted candidates for office—in an effort to put a check on Murray Lenson, they'd both let themselves be talked into running for places on the town council. Now, as they walked back down the hill together, they observed the signs and agreed darkly the day could get worse before it got better.

'Sounds like it might have been a killing, over at the hookshop just now,' Bingham remarked, and Chapman nodded. From the direction of the dingy row of buildings that housed the town cribs, there'd been a burst of shooting mingled with the screams of the women. The tough crowd that made their headquarters at Lenson's were really feeling their oats this morning. Anything could happen.

Chapman said nervously, 'I hope to God Lucy has sense enough to stay off the street!'

'Thought I saw her heading for your office, a while ago, with Mrs. Lavery. They'll be all right there.' The hotelman added curiously, 'How's that new clerk of yours making out?'

'Paul Lavery? Oh, he's competent,' Tom Chapman conceded. 'But he doesn't seem much interested. I have an idea any job would begin to bore him after the first week or so.'

'That's too bad.' Bingham shook his head. 'Appears to be a personable chap. A nice wife, too.’

‘It’s chiefly because of her that I hired him—and because Lee Stormont asked if I couldn’t give him something to help them get by this winter. I’m afraid, if he doesn’t straighten out and start thinking about something bigger than himself, the lad’s headed for trouble . . .’

They had reached the intersection. Starting to cross, they held up as a bunch of riders came bursting out of the side street, lifting dust, shoe irons and palmed six-guns winking back the sunlight. They came shooting at sign boards and windows and the high, cloud-dotted sky. They went by Chapman and Bingham with a rush and a whoop, horses leaning into the curve.

But suddenly one of the riders hauled in, so sharply that his horse dug up great gouts of the powder-dry dirt with its braced forefeet. He pulled the animal around and swung his six-shooter squarely toward Chapman. His teeth showed above it, in a wild grin.

He was drunk, bareheaded; lank hair streamed about his face, and the gun wobbled a little. But Chapman made a big target, and neither of the men on the ground was armed. They stood looking up into the muzzle of the gun and the squinting eyes behind it. Suddenly the fellow roared with laughter; he twirled his revolver, almost dropping it, and went spurring away after his companions.

Bingham said, in a shaking voice, 'That was one of Lenson's crowd. I thought you were a dead man for sure!'

The other had turned a little paler, but he calmly shook his head. 'They don't dare kill either of us. Not if Lenson doesn't want to turn the town against him.'

'Let's hope Lenson realizes that!' George Bingham said hoarsely.

Stormont had slept late, for him, it having been past midnight when he dragged in last night. He did not know when he had been so bone-tired. There were big distances, here in the Outlet, and he was covering them repeatedly—called from one end of the Territory to the other, wherever the many facets of his job took him. With every day that passed there seemed more for him to do—new business to arrange for, branch depots to establish and man; complaints to be ironed out and personnel to break in or fire. Someday this initial flurry would be ended; but it wasn't yet.

He turned from the window of his hotel room which overlooked the street and the dun stretch of land beyond. No rain today, though a few clouds rode before the wind and laid a shuttling of light and shadow across the earth. Listening, he could hear the heightened note in the voice of the town and knew it was because of Election Day.

He had no intention of voting; he didn't consider himself a resident of the town, or even a part of the Territory itself. He had been too busy, he realized suddenly, to think much about the future. He didn't know yet what he meant to do when this job was finished, or where he would go. Vaguely he assumed it would be somewhere distant. He'd thought once or twice of South America. Down there a man should still find uncrowded places, a land that wasn't chopped into quarter sections, a skyline unbroken by the ugliness of sod houses and raw-built towns like Comanche.

Finished dressing, he left his room and started along the narrow corridor that still smelled of pine shavings and fresh paint and varnish. Halfway to the stairs it occurred to him it would be pleasant to have company during his breakfast and, turning back, he went to Lucy Chapman's door and knocked. There was no answer. It was even later than he'd thought, apparently; and chances were, if she wasn't in her room, the girl had already eaten.

He caught himself looking across the hall at the door of the Laverys' room. Perhaps Jean Lavery? But then he frowned at himself. What the hell was he thinking of? You didn't ask a married woman to dine with you!

He supposed the truth was that he still found it hard to accept the fact she was really married—at least to a cross-grained, ornery fellow like Paul Lavery. They were an ill-matched pair; and to Stormont's way of looking at it, she had got very little out of the bargain.

But it was none of his business.

He turned back along the hall and descended the steps to the lobby. The dining room wasn't finished yet; he stepped out into windy sunshine, debating the best place for a meal. Cloud shadows swept the dusty street that lay empty before him, and somewhere a horse whinnied like a trumpet and was cursed by its drunken rider.

Stormont started at an angle across the street. He was well into the middle of it when he heard his name called loudly. 'You son of a bitch!' It was the voice of Lat Roan, belligerent and loud. 'Now you're gonna get it!'

He halted, turning his head, and saw Roan, across the street, standing under the shadow of a wooden overhang. He half-expected to see a gun pointed at him, but at first glance it appeared the man's hands were empty. Conscious of the holster on his own hip, Stormont stood in the windy wash of light and shadow. He called back, 'You sure this is what you want?'

Roan moved out into the sunlight, into the street. Now Stormont could see what he carried in his left hand—a whiskey bottle, half-filled. And when Roan missed his footing in the street ruts, Stormont saw how he threw an arm wide to check his balance.

Roan looked at the bottle, lifted it to his

mouth and with head tilted took a long drag at its contents. Next moment he flung the bottle from him, spraying a plume of amber liquid. It struck a rock and smashed in a sunbright splintering of glass. 'You been askin' for this, Stormont. Always makin' me look small—every time we run up against each other. I'm not takin' it any more!'

Roan was moving as he spoke, though not directly toward Stormont. He had set himself an odd, circling course, that kept the distance even between them; Stormont found himself having to pivot where he stood, in order to face him. It occurred to him Roan might be hoping to pull him around into a position that would have the sun in his eyes. Continuing to turn, he narrowly watched the man's every move; his own hand held close to the jut of his holstered gun, as to a magnet.

'Any time at all, smart boy!'

'Not against a drunk,' Stormont answered coldly.

The redhead cursed him, then, but Stormont wasn't to be goaded. Something in all this seemed to keep slipping out of place, throwing the picture out of focus. He wondered about it, for a count of seconds; all at once, as though a voice had shouted in his ear, he knew what was wrong. There was something studied and crafty in Lat Roan's performance—something that warned Stormont he couldn't possibly be as drunk as he was pretending.

The hour was wrong. It was much too early—even for Election Day. A man just wasn't apt to have taken on quite that amount of liquor . . .

Even as these thoughts were crossing his mind, he realized what Roan had done to him. He was pulled around by the man's maneuvering—almost facing the hotel he'd just left, his back turned now toward the buildings opposite. It was a shuttling of Roan's head that tipped him off. He moved quickly, a sideward leap, and grabbed for his gun even before he sighted the second man standing at the edge of the walk with six-shooter leveled.

They had set him up with childish ease.

The gun was rising in Stormont's hand as that other weapon fired, point-blank. He felt as though his head had blown apart. Then he was on his face in the dirt, hearing a shout of triumph from Lat Roan. He realized he was looking at his own gun looming big at the level of his eyes, a yard in front of him. He tried to reach for it but his hand wouldn't respond. He must have made some faltering movement, though, because he heard Roan cry out, 'He's still kickin'! You didn't finish him!'

That other gun would be taking aim again, and this time there wasn't anything he could do about it. A fog was settling over the street, draining off the sunlight as the strength was syphoned out of his own body.

Then he heard two shots in quick succession, right on top of him; but he didn't feel the bullets strike. Instead, in this last puzzled moment of consciousness, Stormont thought he could hear Bill Ivy yelling, 'Go right ahead, Lat! If you want it, I'll sure as hell give it to you!'

He never heard the answer.

* * *

Paul Lavery, perched at his high desk with a general ledger book open in front of him, scowled at the column he'd just footed and laid aside ruler and pen with a grimace of solid boredom. Shrugging the stiffness out of his shoulders, he looked in deep distaste about the office, resentful of the fate that had placed him here to tot up the records of another man's successful enterprise.

It just couldn't be anything but fate. This was supposed to be the new land, wasn't it—the new Territory where every man was to have his equal chance? But here he sat, in Tom Chapman's office—a nobody, drawing menial's pay from the man who might be the leading power in Comanche before this day was over. It was his wife's fault. After all, he was a city man; but she'd been raised on a farm and she ought to have warned him how tough it would be, trying to make a go of a homestead. If she'd only made it clear, he would have passed up the whole idea and right now he could have owned a valuable business lot, here in what was obviously destined to be one of the important cities of the new Territory. Instead, he sat sweating over another man's accounts—possessor of a half-finished mud house and a quarter-section claim that it became increasingly doubtful he would ever be able to prove up.

He glanced resentfully over at the spare figure of Chapman's chief clerk, Allison, a man with no more ambition than to be content growing gray in the freighter's employ. Yet even this meticulous old man, puttering around now in the big box safe at the rear of the freight line office, was able to give orders to Paul Lavery! And there, by the front window, chattering their heads off, were Jean and old Chapman's daughter.

He flipped a page of the ledger, with savage anger, and was picking up his pen when the shot sounded flatly on the street outside.

Lavery had become inured to such things by now and he didn't even glance up; but then a choked scream from Lucy Chapman lifted his head quickly. Both girls were at the window, staring out into the street. 'What is it?' he demanded, sliding down off the high stool.

His wife answered, in horror. 'It's Lee Stormont! He's been shot!'

Lavery reached the window, with old Allison hobbling up behind him. They had a long and unobstructed view up the street, and though it was nearly a block away they could see everything clearly. That was Stormont, all right—face down in the dirt, unmoving, his hat and gun beside him. Lavery recognized the one who held a smoking gun trained on the fallen man as a hanger-on at the saloon. He saw Lat Roan in the street, a few others were beginning to appear. For one, Elias Rigby, the editor of the Comanche *Intelligencer*, stood in the door of his print shop, stick in hand and leather apron tied around his waist.

As though in a frozen trance, they all looked on as the killer deliberately brought his gunbarrel down, lining up a second shot at his victim.

'You don't want to see this!' old Allison exclaimed as he seized Lucy Chapman and turned her roughly from the window. Paul Lavery's eyes moved to her white and stricken face, and so he didn't witness the second shot fired, or the third. He glanced swiftly back toward the window, in time to see the gunman going down and the big fellow he'd heard called Bill Ivy moving into the scene with smoke dribbling from the muzzle of his gun. Ivy took no more than a look at the man he'd killed. Deliberately stepping over Lee Stormont's body, he advanced on Lat Roan. And Roan dropped back a pace.

There was no way, at that distance, of knowing what they said. Lavery kept expecting to see the redhead make a move for his holster; Bill Ivy's gun was still in his hand, however, and perhaps that stopped him. Now Ivy reached out and gave Roan's shoulder a push. Roan shook the hand aside but he backed farther, and Ivy stepped in fast and this time his shove turned Roan clear around. The hat fell from Roan's head as he whirled back.

For a long moment the two men stood face to face in the sun, staring at each other like two cur dogs. But at the last, it was Roan who backed down before the challenge. He leaned, scooped up his hat, and strode away from there, shoving past a bystander who nimbly moved out of his path.

Next moment, Lavery forgot them all as he saw his wife starting for the door. 'Where are *you* going?' he demanded.

'Out there.'

'No!'

Hand on the knob, she looked at him. 'But it's Lee Stormont! He may be dead!'

'Someone else can see to him.'

Her eyes darkened. 'He's our friend, Paul! One of the best friends we've ever had . . .'

A couple of strides covered the distance between them, brought him to a stand directly before her. He knew that the cold anger welling within him made a stiff mask of his face; he could see it reflected in hers as he looked down at her.

'You're my wife, Jean,' he said. 'I won't have

you making a spectacle of yourself—running into the street after some other man!'

She stared at him as though he was a stranger. He saw the decision firm in her eyes. 'And I won't even answer that!' She turned and opened the door.

His hand closed on her arm. He hauled her around and the open palm of the hand swept across her cheek with a slap that resounded in the quiet office. 'Don't think I'm not aware what's been going on!' he shouted. 'Don't think you've fooled me for a minute—either one of you!'

Her face slowly changed color; the imprint of his hand was plain. Paul Lavery, drawing a ragged breath, became suddenly aware of Lucy Chapman and the old chief clerk, staring.

Jean said slowly, 'You've never done that before! Paul, I could forgive you anything else!'

He tried to speak but his tongue was stilled by the enormity of what had happened. As he stood, unable to move, she turned and walked away from him. The closing of the door had a terrible finality.

Tom Chapman finally located Lenson in a restaurant, seated at a table with Ira Forrester and some of his other well-wishers. Face grim, Chapman moved directly toward them and the loud talk died as he came to a halt beside the table. Murray Lenson put down his coffee cup, looked up with a mocking grin. 'Well, Tom,' he said pleasantly. 'Want to lay any bets on how the election's going?'

'Right now,' Chapman told him in a voice that shook with fury, 'I don't give a good damn about any election. Not with Lee Stormont lying over at the hotel, maybe dying!'

Murray Lenson stopped grinning, but he didn't look at all grieved. 'I heard about that,' he said, wagging his head.

'I'm going to lay it to you fair: Did you send your men to do that job?'

An angry stillness settled in the room. The lids lowered over Lenson's pale eyes. He answered sharply, 'Tom, this sort of thing stops being funny! Nobody lifts a hand around here, but what it's laid at my door!

'No, I didn't send them. I know nothing about it. I haven't even seen Lat Roan today. What I heard, he was likkered up. The other fellow, too. Roan had a couple things in his craw that your friend Stormont stuck there. I'd guess, when they ran into each other on the street, Roan decided to have it out.'

Chapman let a long moment pass silently, as he searched the expression on the other's scowling face. 'That's your story, is it?'

'It's my *guess*!' Lenson repeated sharply. 'If I see Roan I'll be asking him exactly what happened. Meantime, I'd advise you not to go around making charges you can't prove!'

His stare was a challenge, and as he tried to meet it Tom Chapman knew he was getting the worst of this exchange. The knowledge goaded him. He stood uncertainly casting about for a telling rejoinder. But he had no proof—no evidence other than his own galling suspicions, though they were as close to certainty as a man could get.

Someone at the table snickered. The heat of angry blood began to spread up across his throat and face; his hands clenched at his sides.

He couldn't go without a final thrust, however lame. Returning the cold stare of Murray Lenson's pale eyes, he said heavily, 'If Lee Stormont doesn't recover, I'll guarantee now you may wish he had!'

Lemon's upper lip quirked contemptuously. His expression said it was a vain and empty threat. And Tom Chapman took the sting of humiliation with him as he walked out of there.

With the November chill cooling his heated face, he remembered something he'd heard Lee Stormont say once: '*Don't underestimate Murray Lenson.*' He realized he'd done exactly that.

CHAPTER TWELVE

It was Nettie Bingham who told Stormont he had lain unconscious for two days. At first he was incredulous, and then he was appalled. But when he demanded his clothes she proved adamant. 'Nothing doing,' she said. 'Not till I'm sure you're good and ready! In my house, you do as I say.'

'I feel all right,' he protested.

'Don't you know you almost died? Can't take chances with a concussion!'

He lay on his bed in his room in the hotel, watching a patch of sunlight move across the floor as the hours crawled by, and forced to admit he was some distance yet from being as good as new. It was frightening to see how weak he was, to feel the bandage around his head and realize by what margin that bullet had missed taking the top off his skull. So much could hang by such a slender thread . . .

He was ravenously hungry, which he supposed was an excellent sign. He cleaned up every drop of the chicken broth Nettie fixed for him, and thought it a damned skimpy meal for a man who hadn't eaten in two days. He slept again, then. Later on, he had visitors.

The first was Lucy Chapman. She entered after a careful knock, her young face showing such an anxious concern that he tried to make light of his hurt. They talked of small matters, and then suddenly she remembered: 'Oh—Mrs. Yaeger had her baby. A little boy.'

'I guess that's what they were both hoping it would be. How's Mrs. Yaeger?'

'All right, so far as I know. Jean Lavery's

gone out there, to help with things—she'd promised she would, beforehand, and Jody came for her. I knew you'd be wondering why she hadn't been in to see you.'

Stormont said, 'I'd never expect it.'

Lucy looked at him oddly. 'Why, didn't you know? She spent nearly the whole night by your bed, after you were shot. She and Mrs. Bingham and I—we've taken turns.'

He stared, then managed to stammer his thanks. 'I don't know why any of you bothered.'

'You really don't, do you!' Lucy exclaimed, after a long moment.

The hours dragged out their slow length, finding him caught between restlessness and the drained lethargy of his wound. Then big Tom Chapman exploded into the room, a man with his hands full who managed to find a moment he could spare. Sight of him reminded Stormont of something he'd allowed to escape his mind. 'How'd the election come out, anyway?'

'You're looking at the first mayor of Comanche!'

'Congratulations.'

Tom Chapman only shrugged. 'Council just had a meeting, and I was named. Last job *I* ever wanted—but, we couldn't let Murray Lenson take over by default. There's still some fights ahead of us. Somehow, though, we'll get law and order in this town yet!

‘Of course, that’s only the beginning. We got a million things to work out—sidewalks and sanitary regulations and some kind of street lighting, and God knows what all. Council’s met twice already.’

Stormont grinned a little. ‘You supposed to be running a freighting company, along with all this?’

‘It’s sort of a challenge,’ Tom answered seriously. ‘But I couldn’t even try to tackle it without you to lean on.’

‘How’s business? Any more wagons burned?’

‘No. But I lost another account to that fellow McClure. A big one. Afraid they’re beginning to shy away from Chapman Freight.’

‘Well, we’ll do something about that!’

Chapman gave him a careful look. ‘I’ve still got a feeling there’s more than I know about that shooting. Why would those two lay for you, if they weren’t ordered? I don’t like the thought that Lenson might have been trying to hit at me, through you!’

Again Stormont was tempted to open up and tell just what he knew and what he suspected. But he couldn’t, now; for there was Bill Ivy. Bill, who was somehow and to some extent involved with Lat Roan’s crowd, and yet who had defied Roan in order to save a friend’s life. Everything was confused, and the conflict of loyalties tied his hands and silenced him . . .’

He began to feel an impatient urgency, as the pressures and responsibilities of his job began to take over his thoughts again. Alone, he tried to get off the bed but ended up seated on the edge of it, clinging to the ironwork while weakness shook him wickedly. He lay back again, knowing he was trying to push himself too hard. Afterward he drifted again into exhausted sleep.

When he woke, sunset painted the wall of the room in gold. He lay blinking up at Bill Ivy, who stood by the bed, looking at him in silence.

'Hi,' said Bill.

'Began to think you weren't coming in,' Stormont said. 'I wanted to thank you. For saving my life.'

Bill shrugged. 'That's what I was afraid of—reason I didn't come. Hell, I seem to remember you pulling me out of the Canadian, one time. Maybe this squares things.'

'Maybe it does.'

'I'm a sure enough hero now, though! Hey! Look what was in the paper yesterday—right on the front page!' Bill dug into his shirt pocket and brought out a scrap of newsprint, which he unfolded and handed over. It had been torn from the local paper and showed much handling; the story Bill was interested in had been circled heavily in pencil. Stormont, raised on an elbow, held it to a better angle in the sunset glow and read the item, under the heading:

MORE BLOODSHED!

Yesterday we witnessed another daylight shooting on the streets of Comanche. It took place only yards from the Intelligencer's office, and we saw the whole thing.

It was such a common occurrence we almost wonder that we bothered to look.

We saw two men force a third into an unfair fight. We will not mention their names, out of respect for the safety of our own skin, such being the situation in this town. At any rate, they got their victim, or nearly did. If Lee Stormont is now alive and recuperating, he can thank one man. This man's name, we understand, is William Ivy. We saw him walk into a pair of guns, kill one man and send the other (nameless) would-be murderer packing before they could finish the job. It was an exhibition of bravery such as we had almost believed impossible in this decadent time and place.

Comanche now has a city council—a real first step toward law and order in our community. We trust they will soon be hiring someone for the post of town constable. We submit that they might do worse in making a choice than to cast an eye in the direction of this same William Ivy. He has a gun and the courage to use it. This town could use both.

Stormont looked up, an eyebrow quirked. 'Pretty good going, for a dumb cowpoke!'

'It's hogwash and we both know it.' But it was evident that Bill was pleased and impressed. He took back the clipping, folded it carefully and returned it to his pocket. Watching him, Stormont had another thought then that made the smile die on his mouth.

He said coldly, 'How's Lat Roan?'

His friend shot him a glance, under his brows. He was suddenly uncomfortable. 'Look!' he began. 'I know what you're gonna say . . .'

'He helped set me up for a killing. Am I supposed to forget that?'

'He was drunk. And you got to admit you'd been pretty damned rough on him!'

Stormont said: 'Well, he'd better stay out of my way or I'm apt to get a whole hell of a lot rougher! You can tell him that if you want to.'

Bill lifted a shoulder, uneasily. 'Why should I tell him anything?'

'You're a friend of his! Remember?' Suddenly, moved by memories of what the two of them had shared in the past, and by an urgent concern over the trend things were taking, Lee Stormont was almost pleading. 'Look! What's happened to us, Bill? What makes a guy like you run with a crowd like

Lenson's?' And then, after a pregnant pause: 'Or—would it be Hayes McClure you work for?'

Bill Ivy tried to show him a look of honest puzzlement. It didn't quite come off. 'McClure?' he echoed innocently. 'Who's that?'

All the suspicions were hardened, then, into near certainty. For a moment Stormont couldn't trust himself to speak.

He shook his head. 'I won't make you lie to me,' he said gruffly. And, after the briefest of hesitations: 'Bill, why don't we cut loose of this place—you and me? Hit for California or Oregon or someplace they haven't cluttered up too much yet? We could have fun again—like we used to.'

Bill stared for a long moment, trying to read what was behind this. He said finally, 'I don't get it! I figured you was married to Tom Chapman and the freighting business.'

'Just doing a job.'

But lying didn't come naturally to him, and he knew Bill wasn't fooled. The other's frown deepened. 'I don't believe that! You're thinking I'm in some kind of trouble. I do believe you'd chuck everything—throw it all over—on the chance you could get me to ride out of it with you!' For a moment, as this sank in, there was a real closeness between these two. The sacrifice seemed suddenly not to matter—Stormont even closed his mind against the thought of what it would mean to Tom Chapman. His bond to Bill Ivy was an older one and, in that moment, very important.

But then Bill ended it all as he shook his head with a grin. 'Aw, hell! I can't leave. I'm a man of property. Got me that quarter section on Pecan Crick, not even proved up yet!'

And Stormont knew the moment was past, the chance lost. Whatever happened now, from this instant their paths were forking and separating, for good. Slowly he nodded. In a dead voice he said, 'All right, Bill. If that's the way you want it. We'll forget I said anything.'

A moment later, Bill was gone. Golden sunset, that pulsed in the dust-streaked air of the room, turned duller pink and then began fading to gray twilight. Still propped on one elbow in the bed, Lee Stormont stared through the window at the paling sky above the buildings of Comanche.

It was as though something precious to him had been finally taken from him and lost for good. He had never felt so utterly alone.

* * *

Murray Lenson barked, 'Come in!' and scowled as he saw the man who entered. His big, balding head wagged disapprovingly. 'Again?'

Opening the door had made a draft and the

booming, whooping night wind, finding a crack in the jerry-built siding, stirred through the office at the rear of the saloon, causing the flame of the bracket lamp on the wall to gutter and waver. Paul Lavery looked sick in its flickering wash of light. His clothing was disarrayed, his collar open, his sensitive face flushed with drink.

The houseman who had ushered him in said, 'You told me next time, boss, you'd want to talk to him yourself.'

'How much is he in?'

'Eleven hundred.'

Lenson shook his head, whistling sharply under his breath. He dismissed his man with a glance and then pointed to a chair as the closing of the door shut away the saloon noises. 'Sit down.' When the other had dropped heavily into the chair he demanded crisply, 'Well, what about this?'

Paul Lavery pawed the hair out of his eyes with a beaten gesture. 'Damnedest, rottenest luck!'

'Anyone that loses the way you do, should leave the cards alone.'

'What else is there to do with my time? This damned country . . .'

Lenson shrugged. 'Don't bother me with your troubles. All I want to know is when you're going to pay up.' Getting no reply but an eloquent lift of one shoulder, his eye hardened. 'Would you want me going to your boss?'

'Chapman? Lot of good *that* would do you!'

'Your wife, then.'

The young man's head snapped up, his hand tightened on the edge of the desk. 'By God, if you dare—!' But then he subsided, and his mouth twisted. 'It wouldn't matter. She's left me.'

'Left you?' Lenson sounded curious, wholly without sympathy. 'When did this happen?'

'A week ago. She's supposed to be helping out a woman that had a baby—but, I know the truth. It's just an excuse to get away from me and stay gone!' His face worked, his cheeks bunching and his mouth drawing long as though he were on the verge of tears. The other studied him with distaste, seeing a man who'd slipped badly since that first day in the saloon tent, when he'd forced Lenson to break up a lucky run with the dice.

He said, 'You don't like this country much?'

'I hate it! But—I'm stuck.'

'You sure as hell are. For eleven hundred dollars! And you better hadn't try to run out on it!'

'I haven't got anything to run with! You needn't worry. I don't know how, but I'll pay.'

'Damn' right you will!' But Lenson was looking at him with new interest, a vagrant thought crossing his mind. 'You work in Chapman's freight office, don't you?' He pictured the place—the big box safe, the flood of trade that passed through there daily, the steady flow of cash to Chapman's Kansas City bank. Suddenly he found his thought crystallizing into interesting shapes.

Maybe there was an answer here to his problems, and even a way of getting out from under the thumb of Hayes McClure. Somehow, by God, he had to find a way! It was no good, not being his own man. He was no whiskey runner, now. He was a power in Comanche. Intolerable, that he should have to go on being a front for the one who secretly owned this saloon and financed all his operations.

But first of all he had to be sure of his man. 'Maybe we can work something out,' he said pleasantly. 'How about a drink? Looks like you could use one.'

'Why—thanks!' Paul Lavery seemed relieved and more than a little puzzled. The saloonman got a bottle and glasses out of the desk. As he uncorked and poured, he was already studying this fellow—cold-bloodedly, like an instrument he hoped he'd be able to use.

* * *

The freight wagon and trailer had been halted in a shallow gully, where leafless branches of a stand of cottonwood laid an intricate pattern on their canvas coverings. The mules stood in the traces, feed bags in place. The driver and his swamper, squatting by a fire, were cooking up a meal of beans and coffee.

'Sitting ducks!' Lat Roan said in a tone of contempt. He didn't bother dividing up his crew of five men. They rode straight in, Bill Ivy at the leader's stirrup, the pack horses trailing; fallen leaves, brown and crisp, deadened the noise of their coming but at last the old mule skinner looked up, staring. He had a fry pan and a long-handled spoon in his hands; he dropped both into the fire, and as the horsemen reined in he scowled at the neck cloths tied across their faces. Slowly he got to his feet. 'What is this?' he demanded.

He was an old fellow, spare of frame and spry of build—probably three times the age of the smooth-cheeked youngster who squatted beside him. The young fellow looked frightened; but the other was only mad.

'We're taking over,' Lat Roan said.

'Hell you are!' the driver snapped back. 'Nobody ever touched a wagon I was driving!' As he spoke he moved back until his shoulders were placed defensively against the tailgate of the forward rig.

'They are, this time.'

Bill Ivy said, 'Don't give us any trouble, now, old-timer.'

'I'll give you plenty!' The old man flicked him with his scornful stare, and then let it return to settle on the red-headed leader. 'The rag over your face don't fool me, Roan!' he declared. 'Bet I could name a couple of your friends, too. Take 'em and get the hell out of here, or I'll have the lot of you in court!'

Bill frowned behind his own mask. He sensed the stiffening of the man at his side. Lat Roan said, too quietly, 'Kind of a bad mistake you just made, sayin' that!'

'The hell with you!' the old man shouted, and made a sudden twisting lunge and reach across the tailboard of the wagon.

Noon sunlight glinted, dully, from the blued barrel of the shotgun he dragged forth; then a shot crashed in the quiet of the gully and the old fellow doubled up like a stepped-on bug. As Bill Ivy stared, frozen, the swamper started from his place beside the fire. He had a look of horror on his thin face; his hands dangled, indecisively, from the ends of knobby wrists. Bill saw Lat Roan swing his smoking gun around, watched the youngster go down as the weapon smashed a second time.

The horses spooked and were cursed to a stand; the less excitable mules stamped and waggled their ears above the canvas oat bags. Slowly things settled again.

Too late Bill broke loose from his shocked inaction. He turned fiercely on the man with the smoking gun. 'Damn it! Did you have to do that?'

'You saw him go for a gun.'

'But not the kid! He never even had one!'

Lat Roan shrugged, indifferently regarding the two he had murdered. 'His hard luck!' he grunted. 'Couldn't leave him alive after he heard the old man identify me.'

'Like hell! He was too scared to talk.'

'Now, he's too dead,' Roan answered. He shoved his gun back into the holster. 'And that's safer . . . Let's get to work!'

The rest of the job took little time. A single bullet apiece disposed of the mules—this being a part of the chore Bill Ivy failed to understand and vaguely disapproved of, feeling that wanton destruction of living flesh was a distressing thing. But these bore Tom Chapman's brand and so were no use to them; and Lat Roan had definite orders. Bill Ivy let him carry them out himself, taking his own part of the work in the looting and firing of the wagons, the loading of the pack horses.

But his sour and rebellious mood didn't ease from him, and he made no secret of his feeling. Miles away from there, and hours later, when Roan called for a general halt to rest their animals and scan the backtrail for any unlikely sign of pursuit, Bill's silence became painfully obvious. Roan confronted him with a challenge. 'You got a burr under your tail, all right! Maybe you don't like takin' orders from me any more?'

'Not some of your orders, I don't!'

The man's eyes studied him, coldly. 'I don't know,' he said. 'Ever since that little dust-up on Election Day, seems to me you been lookin' for trouble.'

'You just better hope I never find it!' Bill said.

'Maybe you think I'm scared of you . . .'

'You had a chance, that day, to show you wasn't! I did everything but rub your nose in it!'

The other men were holding their breath. Lat Roan fingered his holstered gun; he ran his thumb slowly back and forth along the backstrap of the handle, but he couldn't draw Bill's stare away from his face. Their eyes were locked, the enmity standing openly between them now.

'I can't figure out which it is with you,' Lat Roan said finally. 'Whether it's because I went after your friend Stormont, or you're takin' that newspaper story seriously! Beginning to see yourself as a damned hero or something, just because some two-bit country editor wrote a piece about you!'

Despite himself, Bill was aware of heat beginning to spread up through his throat and face. It made him feel a fool, and it made him angry; for now Lat Roan was grinning, crookedly, as though his guess had been confirmed.

'Go to hell!' was the best Bill could think of to say, and he reined his horse away knowing he had lost that round, stung more than he cared to admit by Roan's sneering reference to the newspaper story.

Afterward, riding again in his stubborn silence, he found himself reaching absently toward the shirt pocket where he kept the clipping. His fingers, failing to locate what they sought for, dug deeper. He realized with a touch of alarm, then, that the paper was gone; he wondered where he'd lost it . . .

* * *

Lee Stormont reined in and looked about him, aghast, his nostrils offended by the smell of death and blood, and the charred timbers and canvas and whatever the wagons had contained. The roan didn't like the smell, either. Stormont spoke to settle it, but in the end he had to dismount and tie the animal to a cottonwood so he could approach the scene of carnage.

The picture was clear enough. He picked up the shotgun where it lay trampled in the dirt, broke it, saw the unfired shells and the shine of the polished tubes. The dead driver had been named Bob Howard, and Stormont had known him as a worthy and salty old man. The swamper he hadn't known, but that made no difference. This was murder—the first time the raiders on Tom Chapman's wagons had extended their killing beyond the slaughtering of mules.

As he stood looking at the desolation,

swearing softly, the slanting afternoon light faded; over westward, a dark bank of clouds had advanced up the sky with the waning of afternoon, and now they had swallowed the sun. A chill wind came across the land. It rocked leafless branches overhead, ruffled the manes and tails of the dead animals, lifted the flap of Bob Howard's jacket.

A piece of newsprint, carried by the wind, came skimming across the ground and flattened itself against Stormont's boot. He stepped back, idly glancing down at it. Then it was as though something had turned rock-hard inside him. He leaned and picked the paper up, willing himself to be wrong but knowing he wasn't.

There could be no hope of mistake. It even had the heavy pencil mark with which Bill Ivy had circled the news story about himself.

CHAPTER THIRTEEN

Jean Lavery heard a horseman approaching the soddy and, in some way she never understood, knew at once who it was. Standing there in the gloomy silence, she lifted her head to listen and was surprised at the quickening of her heartbeat. She looked around; the baby was awake but contented, eying her impersonally from the blankets of its packing-box crib. On the bunk, Martha Yaeger slept. Jean snatched up a shawl and let herself out, carefully drawing the door shut.

There was little light in the morning; the cloud sheet that had come in last night hung low and swollen, and a running ground wind tattered the plume of smoke at the mud chimney, whipped red streamers of dust from the field where Gib Yaeger had been plowing. Clutching the shawl, she stood and watched the rider come in, aware of the swelling warmth of pleasure as she saw it was indeed Lee Stormont.

He lifted a hand in greeting and, pulling the horse in, stepped down. As he stood before her she found herself studying him anxiously, looking for signs of his recent illness. There was a shaved white patch on one side of his head where the hair had barely started growing out again, and a piece of court plaster marking the bullet wound that had nearly done for him. But that seemed to be all.

'Hello,' she said.

'Don't tell me you're here alone.'

'The little girl's around somewhere. Mr. Yaeger and Jody went into town about an hour ago.'

'How's Mrs. Yaeger? And the baby?'

'Oh, just fine. The boy's big and healthy. My main worry is trying to keep his mother from overdoing.' She frowned. 'But, what about you? Are you in shape to be riding?'

A brief smile shaped his lips. 'I seem to be. At any rate I've been out in the field for the past three days—on my way to Comanche, now. This wasn't too far off my course, so I dropped by.'

'I'm glad you did,' she said earnestly. 'I've been worried. I was watching, that day, you know. I saw you shot.'

'So Lucy Chapman told me. She also said you helped take care of me afterward. I been wanting to thank you.'

Before his level gaze, she felt the slight warmth that came into her wind-whipped cheeks. Her eyes wavered, then steadied on his again. 'I was glad to do it,' she said. 'When you fell, I was certain you were dead. For a moment I didn't think I'd ever breathe again!'

'Hold on, now! Don't make it worse than it was!'

She lifted her shoulders, under the woolen shawl that she had drawn over them and crossed upon her breast. 'It just didn't seem fair! You've done so much for everyone. For the Yaegers, and the Chapmans. Yes, and for Paul and me! And then—when you could have used help—you had to face it alone, there in the street. You'll never know how glad I was to see Bill Ivy coming, and—' She broke off, seeing the pain that crossed his face. 'Lee! What is it? You sure you feel well?'

He shook his head quickly. 'It's nothing.'

'I don't believe you!'

Her urgency brought her close to him, and placed her hand against his chest while she searched his face for an answer to the question that bothered her. For a long count they stood like that—their bodies almost touching, the wind buffeting them. And then she saw his eyes darken, felt his chest lift and swell beneath her hand with an indrawn breath. Suddenly his arms were tightening about her, pulling her against the rough material of his canvas jacket.

Beard stubble scraped her cheek. His mouth was pressed against her own, and after a first uncertain moment she was returning his kiss with an eager hunger she hadn't known she was capable of. Her hands slid up his chest and her arms went about his shoulders, as they swayed to the unexpected passion of their embrace.

Then he released her, so abruptly she nearly stumbled. 'I had no business doing that!'

Her hands tightened on the sleeves of his jacket as she shook her head. 'It was my fault. I *wanted* you to.'

'Makes no difference.'

'No. I suppose not. But . . . oh, Lee!' In confusion and despair she came against him and laid her face upon his chest. Then she felt his arms rise about her again; they brought a gladness that was rich and deep, though bittersweet with knowing how hopeless this feeling really was.

It was a moment broken at last by a thread of sound from within the house. 'The baby!' she exclaimed, as the crying took on greater volume. 'I—I have to go . . .'

'Yes,' he said gravely. They looked at each other for a heartbeat longer. Then, because there seemed nothing at all to say, she turned from him and descended the two dug-out steps to the plank doorway. Hand on the latch, she looked back at Stormont over her shoulder. After that she pushed the door open and went inside, and let the latch drop to behind her.

Martha Yaeger, wakening, stirred on the bunk. Jean said quickly, 'It's all right,' and hurried to take the baby up. The moment it felt her comforting touch, it quieted; she could hear the lonely sound of Lee Stormont's horse, moving away.

Her lips moved, forming his name. Suddenly tears stung her eyes and she bowed her head, clutching the warm bundle and engulfed with the hunger to be holding a baby of her own—yes, she admitted it: to hold Stormont's baby! To feel Stormont's arms strongly about her, after the heartbreaking years protecting a weakling husband who had been able, really, to fulfill none of her aching needs.

And then guilt came flooding over her, and left her confused and lost.

* * *

Long after the door had closed, and Stormont ridden out of sight, Paul Lavery sat there in the belt of trees above the soddy and trembled so violently he had to keep a hand clenched on the saddle horn to steady him. He might have ridden after this man he'd caught in his wife's embrace, except he knew he wasn't a good enough horseman to overtake him. But if he'd only had a gun, he really thought he would have been tempted to use it.

As his fury settled, his second impulse was to ride down there and call the woman out of the house and let her know exactly what he'd seen; but thought of another quarrel was suddenly distasteful. It could lead to nothing but recriminations and it couldn't change anything. He stayed where he was.

And to think he'd come here to apologize! Eaten by the emptiness of separation, and by guilt for the blow he'd struck that regrettable morning in the Chapman office, he'd finally discovered courage enough to swallow down his pride and ask to be forgiven; his suspicions had come to seem very trivial to him, since he must admit he'd never really seen or heard evidence of anything wrong between his wife and this fellow Stormont.

Well, there was evidence now—all he could ask for! The rage that made him tremble was tempered by a kind of satisfaction, that he had learned the truth in time to keep from making a fool of himself. Now at least his conscience was clear.

He wrenched his horse's head around with a jerk at the reins that sawed the bit and nearly set it to pitching. Grimfaced, he quieted it and turned again in the direction of Comanche.

One other thing had been settled today: He could quit stalling Murray Lenson! Despite the danger of crossing the saloonman, he'd held back, trying to find another way out of his debts—mainly concerned for what Jean would have thought and said if she knew what he was being pressured into. Well, it was the last time he was going to let *that* bother him!

Nor would he waste sympathy on Tom Chapman. Chapman was going to be hurt—but, he paid Stormont's wages, didn't he? So let him take some of the consequences! Paul Lavery knew his course now, beyond any further debating.

* * *

The big space heater in Chapman's Freight Company office was glowing cherry-red, putting out a wave of warmth to welcome Stormont as he entered. Allison, the chief clerk, greeted him; he nodded in return and agreed it was getting pretty blustery out. But a moody silence was on him and he didn't feel talkative. And then, as he stood holding out his hands to the glowing metal of the stove, a voice from the open door of Tom Chapman's office caught his ear, and sharpened the barbs of his mood.

It was Bill Ivy, saying, 'What about Tilghman?'

'I admit I thought of him,' Tom Chapman answered. 'Some of the federal men are pinning on local badges for extra pay. But he's stationed over at Perry and that means he ain't available for us. Anyway, there's the situation, Bill. What do you think?'

'Well . . .' And then Bill was looking up from his easy sprawl in a chair beside Chapman's desk, as Stormont appeared in the doorway of the smaller office. His white-toothed grin flashed. 'Hi there, boy! Somebody told me you was up and around again.'

'I've been in the field,' Stormont said, nodding to Chapman. He added bluntly, 'What's going on?'

'Me and the mayor's talking official business.'

'Oh?' Stormont couldn't quite keep the steel out of his voice, or the coldness from the pit of his stomach.

'Glad you showed up,' Tom was saying. 'Reckon you know Bill Ivy better than anybody else around. You've always been strong for him. And after what he did—saving your hide for you on Election Day—I don't blame you. I figure him as the man for this job.'

'What job?'

'Town marshal of Comanche. The council's sort of leaving it up to me to find one. A majority of us, at least, know we don't want the man Murray Lenson's pushing—that gunslinger of his, Irv Kinoy. Well, what do you say to Bill, here?'

Stormont's tongue felt leaden. 'Maybe I oughtn't to say anything,' he managed. 'I might be prejudiced.'

'I reckon the mayor's takin' that into account,' Bill said, grinning. 'He knows we're friends.'

'And I'm still asking,' Chapman added.

There was to be no easy way out. 'He's fast with a gun,' Stormont said finally. 'And he's got his share of nerve. If those are the things you're looking for.'

'I'd say they were exactly the things we're looking for!'

To Stormont it seemed apparent that Bill was all but signed up. And it was equally clear, knowing what he did, that he couldn't let this go through. He took a long breath, settled himself. 'He don't need any testimonial from me,' he said gruffly. 'It was all said in the newspaper. Show him that clipping, Bill. You carry it around in your pocket, don't you?'

Bill's hand, as though by instinct, moved up and then paused. 'Why, I—think I left it in my other shirt.'

'I read the piece,' Chapman said nodding. 'Frankly, it's what gave me the idea . . . I've told you the pay, Bill. Reckon the job's yours if you want it. Of course, I'd need a guarantee that you'll stay on at least six months. Rather not have to go looking for another man right away.'

Bill was already nodding agreement. But before he had a chance to speak, Lee Stormont interrupted. 'That's one trouble with Bill,' he said soberly. 'He tends to be fiddle-footed. Always looking toward the other side of the hill.' As he spoke he was reaching into his jacket pocket. He could feel Bill's eyes on him, could see the first puzzled uncertainty warp the shape of the man's grin.

'Oh, I wouldn't say that,' Bill objected, hazel eyes probing at Stormont. 'You know how it is. Man reaches a time eventually when he changes—finds a place he sort of likes . . .'

'Where they put flattering things about him in the paper?' Stormont's hand came away from his pocket now and Bill's eyes flickered and widened suddenly as he saw what it contained. 'I don't know, Tom,' Stormont said. His voice had hardened subtly; its tone brought Bill's searching glance back to his face again, and he met it squarely. 'I just wonder if he's going to be happy, staying around here . . .'

There was a silence, then, in which they could hear the snapping of burning wood in the space heater out in the other office. Bill Ivy stared as though fascinated by what the man in the doorway was holding. His mouth opened, closed again. The healthy color of his sun-beaten face had receded faintly. Tom Chapman, obviously a little bewildered, looked at Bill again. He said, 'Well? It's up to you.'

Another moment, while Stormont turned the folded scrap of paper between his fingers and the room seemed to wait on Bill Ivy's answer. And in that moment, Bill changed. Stormont could see the harsh and angry disappointment settle on him, the resentment that looked out of his eyes as he said, with a hard brusqueness. 'Maybe he's right. Thanks anyway, for the offer.'

Tom Chapman's big head jerked with his surprise. 'Why, I thought it was settled! You mean—the answer is no?'

'You got ears, I reckon!' Bill Ivy kicked back his chair, swept his hat off the desk as he got abruptly to his feet.

'Well! I'm sorry, Bill,' Chapman stammered. 'I—' He broke off. Bill Ivy was already striding out of the little room, shouldering roughly past Stormont and through the door. A definite and hard hostility was in his expression and the swing of his shoulders. His eyes, set straight ahead, would not meet Stormont's.

In the returning stillness, the pair who remained heard the slam of an outer door cut away the solid tread of Bill Ivy's footsteps. Tom Chapman speared the other man with a glance, and his eyes narrowed in puzzlement. 'I just don't understand! Is something going on here that I don't know about?'

'Excuse me,' Stormont said bluntly. 'I got to talk to him!' And he turned away.

Coming out into the main office he asked old Allison, 'Which way did he go?' The clerk pointed wordlessly toward the side door leading to the wagon yard and corral.

As Stormont swung in that direction, the street door opened. Paul Lavery, entering, brought the November chill with him; for just a moment he and Stormont were face to face. Stormont saw the sullen hostility that leaped into the other man's stare, and responded to it with a stab of guilt as he remembered what had happened that morning at the Yaeger homestead. But a more urgent matter pulled at him, and without stopping to wonder at Lavery's expression he strode on to the wagon-yard door and outside, closing it behind him.

At once he discovered Bill Ivy, tightening the cinch on his saddled bay gelding that was tied to a wheel of one of the wagons parked along the high fence. Stormont went down the three plank steps and across the gritty yard. Bill, hearing the grating of his boots behind him, stiffened and he turned, face nearly expressionless.

The look of him started the sick anger welling inside of Stormont. He battled it down, trying to keep a grip on his temper as, halting, he thrust the newspaper clipping at the other man without a word. Bill looked at it. At last he shrugged, and took it. 'All right,' he said bluntly. 'Where'd you find it?'

'I think you know!' Stormont said.

'Why would I?'

It was the attempt at evasion that tipped the scale. Sudden fury took Stormont in its grip and his right fist doubled itself and arced forward, to explode against Bill Ivy's jaw. Unexpected as it was, it caught the man off balance and threw him sideward, against his horse. The animal snorted and stepped away; Bill, pawing at the saddle leather, somehow kept from falling.

He touched a hand to his jaw, let it drop again. 'Now, wait!' he mumbled, and tried to grin. 'Look, boy! You and I have got no fight!'

Deliberately Stormont hit him again. 'Either you fight,' he said, emotion choking him, 'or I take you back in there and give Tom Chapman the whole story!'

Small fires had been kindled in Bill's pale eyes. On braced legs, head shot forward, he glowered at his friend. His mouth twisted. 'The hell with you!' he shouted suddenly, and charged.

They were well matched, as Stormont knew from friendly bunkhouse tussles in the past—about the same in height and reach, with Bill favored by a few added pounds of weight but Stormont having an advantage in slightly quicker reactions. But neither man was interested now in fighting styles. There was a primitive fury in the way Bill Ivy came lunging, and in the way Stormont side-stepped and swung a clubbed fist and forearm down across the side of his neck as he went by.

Bill was driven off his feet and went plummeting, to slide on his face in the grit and dirt. He lay there a moment, stunned. 'Get up!' Stormont ordered. Bill lifted his head, showing a cheek scraped raw and bleeding. He looked at Stormont, who stood waiting for him. Then he put his hands against the ground and pushed up.

'The hell with you,' he said again hoarsely.

Stormont let him pull his feet under him before he waded in. Bill got over a swing that bounced off his shoulder and grazed along his head, waking some of the pain of that recent bullet wound. It stopped Stormont for only the count of a second; then cold anger carried him forward, blocking a second punch and smashing Bill full in the face with one of his own, afterward sending a fist to the chest that drove breath out of him. They came smashing together then and stood toe to toe, battering each other; they fought silently, their shifting boots kicking up dust for the wind to whip away.

Stormont felt his cheek laid open by a glancing blow but the pain was meaningless. All that mattered was the face of the man who had been his friend—the lips pulled back now from clenched teeth, the pale hair plastered down to the glistening, sweaty forehead. Bill's foot turned on a loose stone and in going down he grabbed at the other's clothing, pulling him to the ground with him. They landed rolling, slugging. They tangled with the legs of the saddled horse and it snorted and squealed in panic, lashing out as it sprang clear and narrowly avoiding crushing a skull with an iron-shod hoof.

Bill broke loose and scrambled to his feet. Stormont, reaching, grabbed a boot but tore his hand on the spur. Bill was thrown off stride. He dropped to hands and knees but got up again, with Stormont hard after him. A hand hooked Bill's shoulder, spun him; a blow to the jaw drove his head half around, and then the tongue of a parked wagon chopped him across the knees and he dropped.

Waiting, panting hard, Stormont let him catch a hand over the tongue and haul himself up, before he grabbed and hit him again; this time Bill rolled clear across the tongue and landed, hard, on the far side of it. Stormont vaulted over and, leaning, yelled at Bill to get back on his feet. The other man only stirred feebly; but Stormont wasn't ready to call quits. He leaned, hooked the limp shape under the arms and lifted, to drop him chest-down across the wagon tongue when he realized Bill was beyond further fighting.

He straightened, sobbing for breath, and shakily running a hand across the smear of blood from his split cheek. It was then that he heard the gasp, and lifting his head saw Lucy Chapman standing a few yards distant, both hands pressed to her mouth.

Dully, he stared while his head slowly cleared; and now he recognized the expression on her face, for he had seen it before. It was the same look she'd worn that first, bad night in Caldwell, when she watched the lynching of the sooner. Horror and loathing mingled in her eyes; she shook her head, as though willing what she was seeing not to be true.

It shocked Stormont out of his lethargy, to an awareness of how he must look standing before her—face bloodied and hands bruised from the battle with a man she'd understood to be his best friend. 'Lucy!' he exclaimed; and then, 'Wait!'

But she was already turning, almost running as she hurried away from him toward the clapboard office building. Stormont would have called again but he knew it was useless. Too late to prevent her seeing what she had seen; and he couldn't expect her to understand.

Thought of her was shoved aside as Bill stirred at his feet. Stormont turned back and saw the man groggily pushing up to a stand. This time, there was no fight left in him.

'You bad hurt?'

'Get the hell away!' Bill Ivy fended him off with the thrust of an arm. He sagged down on the wagon tongue and crouched there, weaving a little, blinking and shaking his head.

Stormont's own right hand was beginning to bother him as feeling returned to it; that last blow to the jaw might have done something to it—perhaps cracked a knuckle. He worked the fingers as he looked coldly down at the other man.

'I won't do what I know I ought to,' he said. 'Which is to tell Chapman the whole story. I won't, because we were friends and you saved my life. But this washes us up! Bob Howard was a friend of mine, too. I didn't know the kid, but they both deserved better than murder!'

Bill's wavering stare lifted and settled on him. 'If it makes any difference,' he said heavily, 'I didn't shoot either of 'em.'

'I hope that's true,' Stormont replied. 'But it don't make a hell of a lot of difference! You were there. Or, do you deny it?'

He thought for a moment Bill was going to try; but at last he shrugged and looked away. 'What's the use?'

Stormont considered him a moment. 'It was Lat Roan did the shooting, wasn't it?'

'Think I'd tell you?'

'No,' Stormont agreed heavily, after a pause. 'No, I don't suppose you would—and I don't suppose I'd want you to. But I also know this: I don't want to see you here any more! I'll give you twenty-four hours. If you're still around after that, I'll forget we were ever friends!'

The other man only looked at him, not speaking and not moving from his seat on the wagon tongue. Turning away, Stormont saw Bill's hat trampled on the ground and, near it, the newspaper clipping. He picked them both up and tossed them in the man's lap.

Bill looked at them stupidly for a moment. His mouth twisted and he took the piece of paper in his fingers. 'It's a laugh, you know it? I was beginning to believe this thing! Almost seemed like I'd been mistaken, thinkin' only of myself all these years. What that editor said—it set real good! Made me want to take on that marshal's job—make something useful of myself for once!' He shot an upward glance at Stormont but found no glint of sympathy in the other's face. He gave up then, with a shrug; deliberately he tore the piece of newsprint to shreds and dropped them at his feet. 'But you're right,' he said. 'I'll never change. Except for the worse.'

'Remember,' Stormont told him harshly. 'Twenty-four hours. Then I go to Tilghman.'

Stormont got no answer. He turned and walked away, leaving the fragments of their friendship with the torn scraps of paper scattered on the ground.

CHAPTER FOURTEEN

Paul Lavery, standing behind old Allison with a stack of ledgers that belonged in the big safe, watched him working at the dial and felt a growing anger. The old bastard didn't trust him a minute, made a big thing of keeping the combination a secret from him; try as he might he hadn't once, in the time he'd been working here, been able to catch a look at those numbers past the old fellow's stooped shoulder. He'd assured Lenson this part of the job would be easy, and now he had to admit he couldn't come through. Lenson wasn't going to like it.

The clerk completed the combination and swung the massive door wide. He turned, and frowned. 'Well, who you staring at?' he said sharply. 'Hand them here!' Paul ironed the resentment out of his face, all at once alarmed lest the old man should somehow manage to read his thoughts. Wooden-faced, he shoved the stack of books into the waiting hands.

The inner office door suddenly slammed open and Tom Chapman came tramping out, his face a study in alarm and anger. A small hum of talk had been coming through the closed door for some minutes—his own voice, and his daughter's. Now he said loudly, across a shoulder: 'I'll see about this! I'll find out what's going on, all right!'

'No! No, Pa!' She came running after him. Lavery watched her clutch at her father's sleeve, to halt him. She was distraught, and plainly had been crying. 'You mustn't do that! I—I'd die of shame for Lee to know I came straight to you with what I saw!'

Plainly dissatisfied, he halted, nodding. 'You're right, I guess. It's their own affair, not ours. But I can't help wondering what they were fighting over. Those two were supposed to be the best of friends!'

'It was horrible!' Lucy said.

Tom Chapman stood looking down at his daughter's bowed head and pain cut deep into the lines of his face. Neither seemed to notice Paul Lavery, staring openly. Now, however, old Allison caught his eye and gave him a commanding jerk of the head to remind him of his manners. Paul glowered at the clerk but turned back to his high desk and his endless bookwork.

Chapman said softly, 'I reckon I know how it is, girl. It's no secret to me, the way you've felt about Lee Stormont—even if he wasn't aware of it. What you just now seen must really have come as a shock. But—don't be too quick to blame him, without knowing what brought this on. It's a pretty rough country we're part of.'

'It's a terrible country!' She lifted her head; her eyes were swimming with tears. 'When I came, you said the matter of my staying was up to me. If I tried and found I couldn't—adjust—couldn't make myself fit in—'

'Wait, child!' he exclaimed, with anguish in his voice. 'Be careful! Be sure of what you're saying!'

She shook her head. 'I *am* sure! And I'm sorry, but—I just can't stay here! I can't! Not another day, after—after what I've seen it do to him. I couldn't face him again. I know I'm a coward to run away, but I can't help it. And—you promised!'

'Yeah, I promised.' He raised a hand as though to touch her, but then dropped it again. His shoulders settled, and disappointment had etched new lines into his heavy features. 'And I guess you're right . . . Well, there's still your mother's people, back there in New Hampshire. They were always willing to have you. They ain't close kin; they'll be strangers, but it begins to look like you and me would always be strangers, anyway.'

'I'm sorry, Pa,' she said in a small voice, looking at the floor. 'I really am.'

'So am I. There's the new house—another couple weeks and it'll be just about ready to move in. Gonna seem kind of big and empty. I only built it for you . . .'

'You couldn't have done any more for me than you have! But I'm not worth it! It's just what I said—I'm a coward. Like Mother. She wasn't able to face this country, either.'

Tom Chapman stirred himself. 'Well, I'll get off a letter to your cousins, tell 'em you're on the way.'

'No, Pa. I can't wait for a letter,' she said. 'I want to leave tonight.'

'Tonight!'

'I can't face him again!'

After a long, pained moment, her father sighed and nodded. 'All right. If you're really set on it. I guess it's best got over with! We'll have you on the six o'clock train . . .'

*   *   *

'Tonight?' said Murray Lenson, and scowled. 'That's kind of pushing things!'

'It's the best time, I tell you!' Paul Lavery insisted. 'We'll never have another as good. I mean this! We pull the job now or as far as I'm concerned it's all off!'

Lat Roan, shoulders leaning against the inner door of Lenson's office, straightened with a dangerous look on his face. 'And who the hell are you to make conditions?'

Murray Lenson raised a hand to silence him, his eyes not leaving young Lavery. 'All right, Lat! Let's give him credit for knowing what he's talking about.' The swivel chair creaked as he shifted to a more comfortable position. His boot waggled against a corner of the scarred desk. 'Did you get the combination?'

'No,' the young man admitted. 'I haven't had any luck.'

Roan sneered. 'I figured all along we'd have to blow the damn' thing.'

His mocking tone made Paul Lavery color a little. 'Isn't my fault!' he snapped. 'I did my best.'

'But what good *was* your best?' Lenson was studying the young fellow with his pale stare. 'Ain't sure you've given me anything to pay off that gambling debt.'

'What do you mean, I haven't?' He was really stung. 'Without me, you wouldn't have known what night the safe would have anything in it—or when the office would be empty so you could do the job. Besides, I know the inside of that safe like my pocket. I can lay my hand right on what you want.' He glared at Roan. 'Just try and manage this without me!'

'All right, all right.' Lenson checked Roan with a look. 'But there'd better be no slip-up.'

'If there is,' Paul Lavery said flatly, 'it won't be my doing.'

'Right now, you'd better get out of here. Lat, check the door.'

The redhead crossed to the alley exit, cracked it open and checked to make sure no one would be watching Paul Lavery quit the saloon. Seeing nothing more than a stray cat prowling the trash barrels, he nodded and moved aside. In silence Lavery took his departure; when he was gone, Roan closed the door and turned, scrubbing a calloused hand across his red brush of mustache. 'He needs takin' down,' he said sourly.

'Him?' Lenson shrugged. 'He ain't important. He ain't important at all! Once the thing's finished, he'll be involved too deep to open his mouth.'

'You know damn' well he's expecting a cut!'

'He'll take what I choose to give him—which will be nothin'!'

Roan considered this as he turned the chair Lavery had quit and seated himself, arms folded across its back. The noise of the saloon, at midday, drifted in to them—the boisterous run of talk, the jangling music of a badly played piano, the smash of a whiskey glass.

Lenson said, 'You'll need another man.'

'Already got him picked.' Roan's teeth showed white under the edge of the red mustache. 'He's out there at the bar right now, trying to drink the place up. With a black eye the size of an egg.'

His boss scowled. 'Ivy? I thought you two were at outs.'

'We've had a score to settle, since the day to run!' Lat Roan agreed harshly. 'Except for McClure we'd have settled it by now.' He paused, and his eyes narrowed. 'Any objection if I settle it with him tonight?'

'Suits me. I don't think he's reliable. Even if McClure likes him—we've argued about it. I'd be glad to see him out of the way. But, do you think he'll work with you?'

'It's a cinch. He got into some kind of a row with Stormont and Chapman—Lavery wasn't sure what about. He'll be ripe.'

Lenson shrugged indifferently. 'Go ahead, then. Play it your way.'

'Just one other thing: What about Stormont? I'd feel easier if I knew there wasn't any danger of him getting mixed up in the thing tonight.'

'I've already figured about Stormont. He'll be taken care of.'

'Good!' Roan pushed to his feet. 'I'll go set up Ivy . . .'

Bill Ivy was hunched over the bar with his elbows on the wood and a glass and bottle in front of him. Lat Roan washed the look of raw dislike off his face and was grinning as he slid into place beside him. 'Who'd you lose the fight to?' he demanded.

The other, his face swollen and scabbed with recent bleeding, surveyed him in the bar mirror. His lips moved painfully. 'I told you yesterday—from now on, stay the hell away from me!'

'Take it easy. Lenson's got a proposition for you. There's a piece of cash in it. You can at least talk it over.'

Bill Ivy, scowling, picked up his drink. He studied the glass for a moment, not answering; it would be hard to say what debate was going on behind his battered frown. Then, with a shrug, he drained his glass and slapped it down. 'Hell,' he said, to no one in particular. 'Why not?'

In his room at the hotel, Lee Stormont soaked his right hand in hot water and winced, his cheeks fluttering as he worked the swollen knuckles. The middle one hurt like the devil but he was beginning to have hopes it wasn't broken. He took his hand from the washbasin and kneaded it, deliberately flexing the fingers. He hadn't permanently crippled it in the fight with Bill, but he hadn't done it any good. He knew it would be a long time before the hand would serve him normally.

He was staring sightlessly at the window and the gray afternoon, sick with his thoughts, when the timid knock came at the door. Turning he said gruffly, 'Come in!' and then as an afterthought picked up, with his left hand, the six-shooter he'd laid beside the washbasin.

When he saw Jody Yaeger in the doorway, he put it down again. 'Yes, son?'

Jody came on into the room, staring at the marks of Bill Ivy's fists. 'Mr. Stormont! I guess it was true what I heard—that you was in some kind of a fight.'

'Don't ever lose your temper, Jody,' Stormont told him, with a shake of the head. 'Even when you think you're right. It only leads to things you'll wish hadn't been done.'

'Yes sir,' the boy answered politely, but it was plain he didn't understand. After a moment he remembered his mission and tried again. 'Mr. Stormont, there's a man wants to see you.'

'What man is that?'

'You know, one that runs the livery stable?'

'Ira Forrester . . .' Surprised, Stormont nodded and Jody went on.

'Anyway, he asked if I knew you and I said I did, and he told me to find you. Something he wants to tell you, he said. He give me a whole dollar!' Jody held up the bright silver disc to prove it. 'You reckon it's something important?'

'I don't know.' But Stormont was already reaching for his shirt, a thoughtful frown on him. Remembering the boy, he paused to dig up another dollar and toss it to him. 'Now you got two,' he said. 'Thanks for your trouble. I'll drop down and see what's on his mind.'

Jody, who had never before owned a whole silver dollar, let alone two, could hardly believe his fortune. 'Thanks, Mr. Stormont! Gee! Wait'll I show my pa!' He turned and ran out of the room, clinking the silver; and Stormont slowly resumed dressing, puzzling over this matter. Before he left he strapped his holstered gun in its usual place, but when he checked the hang of the weapon in the leather he grimaced with the pain in his hand.

He certainly hoped it wasn't broken.

The clouds, that had been thickening through the November day, were a low ceiling out of which the wind came shouting and pummeling the town. It had a smell of storm to it, he thought as he shouldered into his jacket and turned in the direction of the livery. The wind stung his cut cheek. Horses at the hitch posts stood with their heads down and tails blowing. The sign above the stable door swung on its hooks.

Ira Forrester stood under the archway, watching for him. Stormont walked directly up to him and said, 'You got something on your mind?'

The liveryman's shifting eyes moved all about the other man, then he jerked his head toward the warm, dark interior of the barn. 'Let's talk back there.'

'Let's talk right here,' Stormont said crisply. 'Where I can see you.'

Shrugging, the other didn't press the question. 'I know you don't think much of me,' he said heavily.

'I don't think much of the crowd you run with!'

The man clawed at his straggle of beard. 'Well, we're even. I don't like you. Or your boss, either, come to that. Act like you been appointed by God or somebody to—'

'You prefer somebody like Murray Lenson,' Stormont cut in abruptly. 'All right. That's your business. What is it you wanted?'

'Quit needling me,' the other said with an attempt at bluster, 'or I might decide not to tell you!' But when Stormont merely looked at him, coldly waiting, the man shifted his shoulders and said, 'It's that fellow, Roan. He was here a while ago, getting his horse. He'd been drinking, and—'

The liveryman faltered. Stormont prodded him. 'So?'

'He got to talking about—about a killing. Seemed to think it was funny as hell to have you taking Bill Ivy apart for it, when all the time—'

Again Forrester faltered, as he saw the look that settled into Stormont's face.

'Did he say a name?'

'I—I don't remember.'

'You better try! Was it Bob Howard?' When he got no answer he grabbed the man by a bony shoulder and felt him squirm. 'Are you saying you heard Lat Roan admit he killed that old man?' And when he saw the other's jerky nod he let him go, his own face drawn into a scowl of puzzlement. 'Why tell me?'

'Look, Stormont!' It came in a rush. 'I never counted on murder. I wouldn't have anybody thinkin' I approve of a thing like that!'

After a long moment, Stormont asked, 'You say he took his horse?'

'That appaloosa he favors. Never said where he was bound for.'

'Was anybody with him?'

'No. He rode out alone.' Ira Forrester hesitated. 'But for that reason I got to thinkin'—I've heard somewhere he has him a woman out on a homestead, a little way west of town. Toward the river bottoms. He goes tomcatting around there when her husband's not home.'

For a long moment Lee Stormont considered. Then he knew he had no choice but to follow up this tip, for whatever it was worth. It would be a real streak of luck if he could manage to get Lat Roan off by himself, where his friends wouldn't be around to help him. He had already waited too long for such a chance!

He left Ira Forrester without another word. He was in the saddle with the town behind him before he remembered his injured hand. He pulled it out of the pocket of his canvas coat and looked it over, flexed the fingers and winced. The cold air seemed to squeeze it as in a vise. He pulled back the tail of the coat and started to pull the gun, then let it go with a shrug. He wasn't fooling himself. That hand was hurt!

He could only nurse it and hope it wouldn't let him down when he needed it.

CHAPTER FIFTEEN

At the edge of town he had found fresh sign that could only be the appaloosa, and it was following wagon tracks in the general direction Forrester said. Lat Roan had less than an hour's start and Stormont felt no concern about losing a trail that recent; he held his own mount back, not wanting to risk running it too hard. And again, if he hung too close Roan might get wind of someone trailing him and perhaps try an ambush.

Taking his time, with a steady gait that ate up the miles, he could see on every hand what the September invasion had done to the Cherokee Outlet. After two months, the face of this land would never be recognizable again. Sod that was locked by the grass roots of centuries had stubbornly resisted the plow, but once yielded there could be no restoring it. Lee Stormont wasn't at all convinced this prairie would ever support a farm; but, at any rate, the experiment was being made. By the rules, ten acres of each quarter-section claim had to be under cultivation within six months; and from the saddle he could see the strips of tilled red earth that helped to impose the checkerboard pattern of agriculture upon untamed prairie. Spotted across the land were the soddies in varied stages of completion, and the wells that had been dug, and even an occasional start at fencing. Along the section lines, wagon tracks were already making roads.

In two months, Stormont had grown accustomed to the changes; he found it hard to remember things had ever been different. The herds of longhorn cattle from three years ago seemed a dim memory of some far distant time and place. He scarcely knew what he felt any more. He was often surprised to catch himself thinking in terms of the probable transport needs, when winter ended and the Strip swelled to its full population. He was beginning to think like a freighter instead of a cattleman; which wasn't odd. You became what you lived with . . .'

The run of his thoughts broke as the trail took him to the top of a bushy rise, and the ground beyond dropped away toward a gray and sluggish river. In the middle distance he saw a sod house the color of the ground it sat on. Smoke from a mud chimney was frayed and battered by the same winter wind that combed the long grass growing on the roof, and scudded swollen storm clouds leadenly across the river bottoms.

The door was closed. The horse that stood on trailing reins in front of it was Lat Roan's appaloosa.

He sat for a long time staring at the place. The door remained closed; nothing moved except the plume of chimney smoke, and the horse that stamped and fretted in the wind. If Roan was in there, preoccupied with a woman, there should be little trouble in walking up on him and taking him. And yet, something he couldn't exactly put a finger on bothered Stormont and held him where he was.

It was the horse, he decided. Why didn't the man have it out of sight, since there was always a chance the woman's husband might return? Tied there, a clear identification, it seemed uncomfortably like bait.

Stormont spoke to his own mount and pulled it aside, beginning a slow and wide circling. He kept to whatever natural cover he could find, meanwhile maintaining a careful watch on the silent building. He brought a side wall of the house into view, with a window covered by a wooden shutter. He reined in again, and finally dismounted. He tied to a sapling bole, and drew his gun. The joints in his swollen hand protested as they closed around it.

Slowly he lowered himself to a crouch and then left the protection of the timber, moving crabwise. A wagon box had been removed from its running gear so the latter could be worked on. Stormont kept this between him and the house as he scuttled forward, and bringing up behind it he peered again at the shuttered window. From here to the house he would have no protection.

He was sweating inside the canvas jacket, feeling the warm run of moisture down from his armpits and across his ribs while his face, still raw from Bill Ivy's fists, was chafed and roughened by the winter day. He tightened his grip on the gun, then suddenly lunged up and forward—around the end of the wagon box, straight toward the house.

He was still a dozen feet away when the wooden shutter all at once slammed wide. He saw the gunbarrel thrust across the sill and dropped, rolling, as though he had been tripped. The gun cracked loudly; the bullet must have missed, because he didn't feel it. Earth and sky spun and then he rolled to his feet and saw the vague blob of the face in the window and threw a shot at it. The man pulled back, and this gave Stormont time to make the last few running strides and bring up flat against the side wall.

Gun smoking in his hand, he waited for a target. He thought he heard a brief scurrying inside the house but wasn't sure. The window gaped open and empty. He started inching toward it, the tang of gunpowder in his nostrils.

Still nothing inside the shack. Stormont ducked under the window, straightened on the other side with gun lifting and ready to risk a shot into the room.

A sound behind him made him whirl. He hadn't heard the plank door open, or Lat Roan moving along the front of the house to the corner. Except for the grind of a pebble underfoot he never would have avoided the bullet in his back. But he got around, and he threw himself flat against the wall just in time.

Afterward he could have sworn he felt the muzzle heat and the bullet's concussion, whipping past him. He was bringing up his own gun, in the same instant. He saw the shape of the other man—the high, oddly deformed shoulders. He had a moment to realize something was wrong, thinking, That's not Roan! Then he squeezed the trigger, sending a stab of pain through his injured hand. The gun roared and bucked and knocked his elbow against the dirt wall behind him. The man at the building corner jerked and dropped his gun, his hands hung limp in front of his chest. He sagged against the corner of the building and slid lifeless to the ground.

In stillness then, except for the whip of wind in grass growing on the roof, Stormont turned for a quick look through the open window. No woman inside there—no one at all. Switching his gun to the left hand to ease the pain in his right, he walked over to look down at Irv Kinoy's lifeless face. As he did, puzzlement gave way to anger.

'That damned Forrester!' he said aloud. 'He lied!'

He'd been neatly tricked, all right—lured out here, to what was supposed to have been an ambush. But it was another thought that really bothered him, a vague feeling that there must be some reason why they'd wanted to pull him away from Comanche at this particular time. It was only a hunch, but he knew he'd have to act on it.

* * *

Lacking a regular council chamber, the men who made up the elected governing body of Comanche held their meetings in an unused storeroom belonging to the storekeeper, John Weiss, who was one of its five members. They were meeting there today, in the cold gray waning of a winter afternoon.

For Tom Chapman, distracted by his own emotional problems and his approaching loss, the meeting was an hour of torment that he would have put off if the press of business before the council hadn't been so great. He saw sympathy in the eyes of his friend George Bingham, and something in Murray Lenson and the liveryman, Forrester, that he might have read as an odd triumphant waiting, had he been in a mood to analyze it or to care.

He had to report that Bill Ivy, approached for the job of constable, had for an unexplained reason turned it down. Lenson, who seemed to find this amusing, quickly suggested that Irv Kinoy be offered the job. Scowling in distaste over the name, Bingham put a motion that the matter be postponed for later decision. Weiss and Chapman both supported him and so the matter was temporarily shelved by a vote of three to two. But it was going to have to be faced sooner or later, probably at the next meeting. And then the two elements in the council would most certainly lock horns.

For the moment, there were miscellaneous but pressing decisions that had to be reached. As the moments fled and dim light leaked out of the day, a bill for $61.20, for digging the town well to a depth of thirty-four feet at an agreed rate of $1.80 a foot, was allowed, and $27.75 appropriated for the purchase of a pump. Bids were opened for the construction of public sidewalks and the low bid of twenty-three cents a foot accepted. Other business details took their place on the agenda, were debated and settled. Tom Chapman's manner grew increasingly abstracted until Murray Lenson said at last, with pointed irony, 'If our mayor has more important things on his mind, maybe we ought to cut this short and try some other time.'

Chapman didn't rise to the needling. He glanced at his silver watch and nodded. 'I think we've done enough for today,' he said. 'Tomorrow afternoon all right for everyone?'

The meeting broke up. As Chapman was shrugging into his coat, Bingham came to him in sympathy. 'Maybe she's changed her mind,' he suggested. 'Maybe she won't really go.'

The older man shook his head. He settled the collar of his coat, pulled on his hat. 'She's going. This was building, a long time. Something happened today to settle her mind. She ain't going to change it.'

'Sorry, Tom. I've got real fond of that girl,

myself; so has Nettie. Reckon we're going to miss her, near as much as you will!'

Lenson and Forrester stood by the door discussing something. Their eyes slid in veiled interest to Chapman as he went out into the deepening dusk. If he had seen their faces he might have wondered.

The wind had dropped away and the air was softer, with the smell of snow. To Chapman, the raw buildings of the town under the low ceiling of clouds and nearing darkness looked as drab and unlovely as they must have to his daughter.

And then, nearing the hotel, he saw her luggage piled waiting on the porch beside the door, and knew now that she had not changed her mind. She was really going.

* * *

Paul Lavery, fidgeting at his desk, was approaching a state of nerves. He knew a drink was what he needed, but that was out of the question. His attention was divided between the street outside, the clock on the office wall, and the maddeningly deliberate movements of old Allison as he moved around, filling inkwells and trimming lamps and tending to the other insignificant details that he set so much store by at the end of a day. Damn the man! Would he never leave?

A buggy rolled down the street, passing

outside. Craning for a look through the darkening window glass, he saw the two people on the seat. Chapman and his daughter, already leaving for the railroad station. He looked again at the clock and suppressed a groan. Nearly six, and still that old bastard Allison pottering around, as though he didn't have any home to go to . . .

At that moment the old clerk said, 'I'm getting ready to lock up, son.'

Paul Lavery twisted about on the stool, ran a hand through his hair. 'I still can't find that seven-dollar error,' he said with feigned disgust.

'Let it wait till morning. When your mind's fresh.'

He shook his head. 'I do that, I'll never get caught up tomorrow. I better stick it out. I'm narrowing it down—I'm bound to find it in another hour.'

Allison hesitated, then nodded; his manner said he would never be one to discourage a young man with ambition enough to work overtime. 'All right,' he said. 'Be sure and bank the stove and leave the lamp turned down. You know how to set the latch on the door, I guess.'

Another delay, while the old man pulled the window shades to suit him, checked the draft on the hearer and—his last ritual each night—tested the handle of the huge safe. Then, with a final, 'Good luck,' he was gone. And Paul, in a sweat of haste, barely was able to wait till the sound of his footsteps thinned out in the dusk.

Paul Lavery quit his desk at once, pausing at the street door to throw the lock. After that he hurried to the side entrance and cracked the panel open. He listened for sound in the wagon yard; hearing none, he stepped through, leaving the door open.

Parked wagons stood like ghosts in the early night. Young Lavery's legs shook so he thought they wouldn't carry him the length of the yard to the gate; his hands trembled as he raised the bar that held it closed. Lat Roan was already cursing as he shouldered through, carrying a bundle wrapped in burlap. 'Damn it to hell,' he complained. 'Leave us standing out there where anybody could have caught us!'

'They didn't, did they?' Paul retorted gruffly. 'Nobody hangs around this time of night.'

Bill Ivy had followed the redhead into the yard. 'Let's hurry it up!'

Roan glanced at him, then threw a question at Lavery. 'Did you get the safe open?'

'What do you mean? I told you once I couldn't!' He saw Roan's mocking sneer, and flushed in spite of himself.

Lat Roan jerked his head at Bill Ivy. 'Time's running short. You keep a lookout,' he ordered. 'And a good one! Me and the kid have got work to do . . .'

The northbound was late—delayed, the station agent said, by a hotbox somewhere south of Enid. Chapman led his daughter inside, out of the chill that lay upon the early night. The station was small, with a few benches for comfort and a pot-bellied stove glowing in a cinder box. Beyond the partition, the chatter of the telegraph key rattled intermittently in the stillness.

There were no other passengers waiting for the train. Tom Chapman took care of the luggage and buying the ticket; returning to Lucy he found her waiting on one of the benches, carpetbag at her feet and hands folded primly in her lap. Looking at her, Chapman realized with a pang that she had become again the frightened girl who had arrived in Caldwell, those weeks past. She had started to change, had grown warmer and freer; now, in a matter of hours, she was once more withdrawn into her private world of fears and timidities.

Standing before her, he had to say something. It came out lamely: 'I hope you'll have a good trip. You've got a long way to go, and with all those changes to make—Kansas City, and Chicago—'

'I'll be all right.' She spoke without looking up. Tom Chapman was stung into sudden hopeless rebellion at the way things had turned out. 'Honey!' he cried, flinging out his hands. 'Is there anything at all I can do? Anything I can say?'

She lifted her head; her eyes were

swimming with pain. 'Please, Pa . . .'

He turned away. 'I'm sorry! Said I wouldn't push you, but, I reckon this is the worst night of my life, since—' *Since your mother left!* It almost came out, but he had the strength to hold it back. He was wondering how he could live out these next interminable minutes of waiting, when the explosion, muffled by distance and intervening walls, suddenly rolled across the town and rattled the station windows.

They stared at each other. Lucy said, 'What in the world—?'

The door was flung open; the station agent thrust his head in, his eyes staring. 'Mr. Chapman! Sounds to me like that came from the wagon yard!'

'By God, you got to be foolin'!'

A dozen strides carried him out onto the cinders, shoving the man aside. He looked into the darkness, seeing nothing, hearing the first yelling of excited questions. Something fine and cold filtered down across his cheeks and clung in his lashes and he realized with half of his mind paying attention that the expected snow had silently begun.

Lucy's voice followed him. 'Pa! What is it? What's wrong?'

He didn't wait to answer.

* * *

Pete Quilter said harshly, 'Give me a whack at this guy. I'll make him talk!'

'He'll talk,' Lee Stormont said.

Shoulders pressed against the wall, Ira Forrester trembled and stared from one to the other. 'Don't!' he cried. His face looked yellow in the glow of the lantern hanging from a nail on the stable wall; the smell of fear on him seemed nearly as strong as the warm, ammonia smell of the horses in the stalls. He looked for escape, toward the door where the first straggling flakes of long-expected snow were beginning to settle through the early night.

He took a step toward escape, but Lee Stormont seized him roughly and flung him back against the wall. 'You're going to admit you had orders to send me into a trap!'

The man writhed in fear. The beard fell in a fan across his chest. 'You know I wouldn't do a thing like that!'

'We know you're Lenson's man—he owns you, same as he most likely owns this livery stable. Maybe you figured you had to do as you were told. But he and his men have done murder before and they tried to do it again today. If you've got any sense you'll cut loose while there's time!'

'I don't know what you're talking about,' the man said sullenly.

Stormont and Pete Quilter exchanged a look. The big yard boss, just in from Caldwell, had hailed Stormont on the street as the latter entered town with Kinoy's body tied across the saddle of the appaloosa. He was indignant over the ruse that had narrowly cost Stormont his life. He asked, 'Now what?'

'I'll take it to the federal marshal,' Stormont answered. 'Bill Tilghman's going to be interested.'

'Have you stopped to think—Roan don't like you much. This might have all been his doing, and not Murray Lenson's.'

Stormont shook his head. 'In that case he wouldn't have sent Kinoy or anyone else to finish me off. It's a pleasure Lat would want to save for himself!'

'Then why didn't he?'

'That's what our friend's going to tell us.' He looked menacingly at the stable owner.

'Now, wait!' The man's courage had turned brittle. 'Nothing was said to me about a killing! I swear it wasn't! You were just to be got out of town for a few hours!'

'And then?'

'Hold it!' cried Pete Quitter, a hand lifting. '*Listen!*'

The sound of the explosion had been almost covered by Forrester's frightened whimpering. Now, in a sudden quiet, they stood looking at the snow that sifted past the doorway, straining for a repetition of the sound.

'What do you think it was?' Quitter asked in a hushed voice.

'Keep an eye on him!' Stormont indicated Forrester with a jerk of the head. Not waiting for an answer, he was already hurrying into the dusk.

CHAPTER SIXTEEN

For a moment after the safe blew, Bill Ivy lay prone with the concussion punishing his ears. Damn, but Lat Roan had used enough power to blow out the side of a building! He lifted his head, looked through swirling smoke and saw the door of the big iron box half off its hinges. At the same moment Roan was on his feet and calling hoarsely for speed. 'Get to work,' he ordered Lavery. 'Let's get this cleaned out. You, Bill, on the door!'

Still a little stunned, Bill picked his gun off the floor and took his place where he could watch the street. At first he could see no reaction out there; Comanche lay silent under the increasing fall of snow. But the alarm would spread quickly enough, and he listened for it against the small, hasty sounds Roan and Lavery made as they rifled the contents of the safe.

A shadowy figure moved beneath a wooden awning across the street. Bill's hand tightened on the gun; he called a warning: 'Cut it short!'

'That's good enough!' Across the room he

saw Roan straighten, a bulging burlap sack in his hand. 'Let's get out of here!'

'Wait a minute!' Paul Lavery's protest stopped them both. 'You're forgetting . . .'

'What?'

'You're supposed to tie me. I've got the rope ready. Otherwise they're bound to know I was in it!'

Roan hesitated, scowling at the delay. Near the window Bill saw other figures running in the street and he said tensely, 'Make up your mind quick!'

'All right.' Roan shrugged. 'Turn around,' he told Lavery. 'Your hands behind you.'

He was already pulling his holstered gun as Lavery turned his back. Bill saw the gun arm lift, and winced as it dropped sharply. He saw Lavery buckle at the knees and go down without a sound. 'That takes care of *him*,' Lat Roan said. And then he looked at Bill.

'He ain't gonna thank you for that, when he wakes up,' Bill Ivy said.

Roan didn't answer. The turned-down lamp, shining across his eyes, struck a feral light in them that Bill had seen before. He recognized, too, the odd cant to Roan's head; it was swiveling to the right, the eyes staying fixed on Bill, the lips pulled back until the white teeth showed between them. The gun that had smashed Paul Lavery's skull was turning in Bill's direction.

A flip of the wrist brought Bill's own

weapon swinging over. Roan saw it pointing at him and he froze. Bill shook his head, a wicked impulse riding him. 'Weren't thinking of using that on *me*?'

For a timeless moment they faced each other. Bill knew beyond any doubt he'd read the other's intention, and only his right guess and his quick movement had stopped Roan. The guns gleamed in the lamplight. Bill Ivy, growing impatient, said, 'I been waiting for a showdown. Go right ahead if you feel lucky!'

A shout from the street outside settled the matter. Roan's head jerked. Then his mouth quirked and he grunted, 'Later! This ain't the time . . .' Swiftly he turned away to the side door into the wagon yard. He had to drop the burlap sack a moment while he fumbled at the knob. He flung the door wide and lunged through.

In the same moment, boots struck the front steps. Bill, spinning, saw a figure bulking obscurely beyond the door window, and without thought he fired. In a smash of shattered glass he recognized Tom Chapman even as the latter took the bullet and fell backward into the street. Bill cursed his own hasty reactions; after that he was turning to follow Lat Roan.

* * *

The snow fell thicker with every passing

moment, as night settled over Comanche—even in the gathering darkness, a man could dimly see it dropping around him, and not only when he happened to catch it against the light.

Lee Stormont felt its many fingers brush his face as he stared across in horror at Tom Chapman, sprawling in the street where the shot from within the freight office had dropped him. No time to learn whether he was alive or dead. Stormont didn't join the excited and yelling townsmen who were beginning to gather, now, running up out of the darkness. He held his gun in his left hand, sparing his injured right, while his thoughts raced.

Whoever had shot Tom wasn't going to try that street door. The other way out was the side exit through the high-walled wagon yard, that had a double-leaf gate fastened by a drop bar on the inside. With an urgent sense that there was little time, he swung and went at a run toward the head-high wooden fence circling the yard. He rounded the corner, approaching the big gate. In the darkness, he felt along it and instantly discovered that the gate stood open.

He considered, eyes narrowed. At this time of evening the gate was always closed; the thought crossed his mind briefly that only treachery could have lifted the bar and opened it. He looked at the ground, saw it beginning to shade into faint whiteness with the continuing fall of snow. Not enough yet to have taken a print. Whoever he was after could be penned up in the yard, or already escaped.

Stormont slipped inside and pulled the gate to and dropped the bar in place, with a sound that seemed to him enormously loud. Yonder, at the barn, a kerosene lantern on a pole cast its weak light over the yard. Against this the big freight wagons stood faintly visible, two lines of them along the fence and a third one down the center of the yard. The soft snow sifted down, gentle and silent. The cold worked at a man's cheeks and wrists.

In the barn, a mule stomped a couple of times. The door of the office stood open; a lamp glowed there. Between him and the building, nothing moved.

He thought suddenly he'd heard the scrape of a bootsole, somewhere forward. Listening tensely, he failed to hear it again. He switched his gun to his aching right hand, in readiness. He knew he shouldn't leave this position near the gate, but he felt too helplessly exposed here. So, moving quickly, he gained the corner of the nearest wagon and stood there a moment, his gun hand resting its burden on the cold, broad tire of one wheel. Impatience and a heady sense of danger beat high in him. He knew there was someone near him in the darkness, someone who must have heard the closing of the gate. Out in the street voices were shouting. Whoever was cornered here in the yard would have to make his move shortly.

Losing patience, he called sharply, ‘I haven’t got all night, and I don’t think you have either!’ A gun flared, its roar oddly muffled in the cottony fall of snow. He whipped up his own revolver and fired at the flash, heard a quick break of running footsteps. He went in pursuit, along the lines of wagons that were parked each with its tongue thrust beneath the running gear of the one in front of it. But then he halted, the light of the lantern showing him he’d lost his target, and belatedly realizing he could let himself be drawn away from the gate and so give the fugitive a chance to escape.

He hauled up, uncertainly. He turned, and had started to retrace his steps when he heard a voice he recognized, in astonishment, as that of Bill Ivy: ‘Lee! *Watch it*!’

Pivoting, he saw them both. Lat Roan had moved out of his hiding place behind one of the wagons in order to get a clear shot. A half-dozen yards beyond, Bill Ivy stood spread-legged, arms hanging motionless, watching. Lantern glow gave Stormont the whole picture, in the instant that he was lifting his own gun.

Roan fired but what should have been an easy shot for him was lost in Stormont’s hurried turn. Boots slipping in the snow, Stormont was carried to one knee; there he tilted the muzzle of his gun and triggered. The kick of the gun against his injured hand knocked the weapon from his fingers and dragged a shout of pain from him. The gun fell, spinning, a yard from him; he made no move to retrieve it, but knelt nursing his aching hand and watching Roan.

Hit squarely, the man was thrown hard against the big wagon wheel. His hat fell off, his whole body seemed to sag. He caught at the wheel with one hand and somehow clung there. He still had his gun and he looked over at Stormont, seemed to search and fail to find him. His head turned then; he was looking for Bill Ivy. The gun swung and fired at the man whose warning shout had cost him his life. Before he could see whether the shot was good or not, Lat Roan lost hold on the wagon wheel. He dropped his gun into the scurf of snow and fell upon it, the way a tree falls.

By then Stormont had his feet under him again. He picked up his gun, walked over to look at Roan. The man was dead, no doubt of it—and underneath him, silver and greenbacks spilled from the mouth of a burlap sack. Wasting no time here, Stormont went to where Bill Ivy lay on his back, still breathing with a bubbling effort. Stormont knelt and opened his coat, and saw the spreading stain that was black in the lantern light. He said hoarsely, 'Bill!'

The hurt man stirred slightly; his *eyes* opened. He spoke with an effort. 'Lee? Thought the son of a bitch had got you, sure!'

'You yelled just in time.' Over at the freight office, he could hear the crash as the bolt on the street door gave, and then excited men were tramping through the place; in a moment they would be here in the wagon yard. 'Quit trying to talk. We'll get you inside, and—'

He was getting leverage to pick up his friend in his arms, when Bill shook his head feebly. 'It's no use. He got me good!' Stormont, after the briefest hesitation, knew he was telling the truth and that it was wrong to torment him by moving him. A great grief welled into his throat; his arms tightened around his friend, holding him as he might have done to comfort a hurt child.

Bill was going fast. His lips were moving again. 'Those raids—you were right, boy. It was Roan's outfit.'

'You were in on 'em, then?' Bill's nod confirmed it. 'Working for Lenson?'

'Not Lenson.' Bill spoke hoarsely. 'He ain't got a dime. That guy McClure backs him in the saloon—uses the gang Lenson put together for him.'

'To break Tom Chapman and take over his business . . .'

Stormont couldn't keep the iron out of his voice. Again he felt Bill's head move feebly, managing a nod. 'Guess you're kind of—disappointed in me . . .'

In that moment, Stormont could feel no censure—nothing but a deep loss, that was settling heavily through him and leaving him numb. He shook his head. 'It was your life, Bill.'

'I didn't owe Chapman nothin'. Figured the freightin' business was only a job, far as you was concerned. Found out too late—it wasn't.' He added painfully, 'But at least I quit, after that killing yesterday.'

Was it only yesterday? So much had happened, time was meaningless.

'Don't look to me like you quit!' Stormont said harshly.

'I quit McClure,' the hurt man insisted, so earnestly it brought the sweat streaming on his face. 'This here was Murray Lenson's doing. He hates McClure's guts. Knocking over Chapman's safe was supposed to make it so he could—tell McClure to go to hell.'

'But why'd *you* get in it?'

Bill shrugged with an effort. 'I was sore at the world—losin' that marshal's job. I wanted out of the Strip. Needed travelin' money. But I know now—they never meant me to live through this . . .'

His breathing was heavier, harder. Dimly Stormont was aware that other men stood near, legs and boots circling this spot where Bill Ivy lay dying. One of them came now carrying the lantern from the barn post, and the dancing circle of light set the shadows bobbing as he brought it on the run.

Stormont saw now that Bill was groping

toward the pocket of his bloody shin. He reached inside for him and brought out what he found there, a piece of paper. Bill nodded. His fingers trembled working at the paper, trying to unfold it. 'Like you to have this, if you got any use for it.' His voice was horribly and painfully weak and effort-ridden, now. 'That quarter section on Pecan Crick. Never did—sell the relinquishment. Good piece of land . . .'

The voice ended. The hand stilled. Lee Stormont took the paper from under the cold fingers, looked at it blindly. Then his head lifted and he stared around at the grim faces in the circle of lantern light. He said, 'You heard all that?'

Sober and angry eyes met his. One of the men was Elias Rigby, the editor of the *Intelligencer*; he nodded and said, 'Every word.'

'Good!' Stormont let Bill gently down and pushed to his feet. He walked over to Lat Roan's body and picked up the burlap sack. He scooped in the money that had been spilled, dropped it inside and twisted the mouth of the sack. He looked around again at the bodies.

Somebody said, 'We'll take care of them, Stormont.'

'Thanks.'

He crossed the snowy yard to the office, and part of the crowd followed him. They didn't talk about the thing they had just seen and heard.

The freight office was crowded. Near the gutted safe, George Bingham straightened from examining Paul Lavery's motionless form. He saw Stormont and shook his head. 'Dead. Somebody fetched him a hell of a wallop—smashed his skull. Probably never knew what hit him.'

Stormont, looking at the crumpled shape, found a trace of doubt. He tracked it down, remembered wondering who had opened the gate and let the thieves into the compound. But if there was an answer here, he suddenly didn't want to know it. He turned instead to the old clerk, Allison, who was examining the rifled safe with an expression of dismay. 'I think you'll find everything here,' he said, and handed over the burlap sack. 'Better make a count, and then see if you can find a place to put it temporarily.'

'There's some room in my safe at the hotel,' Bingham suggested. 'I can keep the cash for you, at least. The other stuff I guess will take care of itself.'

'Work it out between you,' Stormont said, impatient to get on to other matters. He looked around. 'Where's Tom?'

'They took him back in his office,' Bingham said. As he turned away, Stormont heard the long wail of a departing train whistle. And at the same moment he saw someone pushing through the crowd, and heard Lucy Chapman crying, 'Pa! Oh, Pa!'

She'd lost her pert little hat; white of face, hair disarranged, she would have fought through to the door of her father's office if the crowd hadn't made way for her. Following, Stormont saw Tom Chapman seated at the desk and someone working over him, doing a crude job of bandaging a wound in his chest. Tom's face was tight with pain, but it slackened incredulously as he saw Lucy among the crowd. He spoke her name, and that brought her around the desk to go down on her knees beside him. She was sobbing; her face was streaked with tears as she exclaimed, 'I love you, Pa! Oh, don't die!'

The man who was working on Tom said, 'Ain't all that bad hurt, Miss Chapman. Bullet scraped a couple of ribs. He's gonna get all right.'

She clutched Tom's brown, hard hand in both of hers, pressed it against her cheek. 'And I'm going to take care of him till he does! You hear me, Pa? I didn't really mean it! I couldn't ever leave you. When I heard the shooting start, I nearly died. I knew everything, then!'

Tom Chapman stroked her hair, that had snow caught in it. He said, over and over, 'It's all right . . . it's all right . . .'

Lee Stormont's face felt like a cold mask as he turned away from the door. He saw George Bingham looking at him, and Rigby and the other men who had heard Bill Ivy's dying confession. They were watching expectantly, waiting for a sign.

Instead, he heeled about and walked alone, out into the snowy street.

CHAPTER SEVENTEEN

They followed him out, almost a dozen of them. Stormont turned impatiently as George Bingham grabbed his arm. 'Don't be a damned fool, Lee! You can't handle it alone. There's still that crowd Roan traveled with.'

'Tom wouldn't have asked anyone to fight his battles,' Stormont said coldly. 'Neither do I.'

'It's our battle. The town is rotten to the core, if Lemon gets away with this!'

'Maybe we know it was Lenson,' Stormont pointed out, 'but we've got no proof for a court. We could only repeat what Bill Ivy told us, and the law would call it hearsay.'

Bingham looked around at the silent faces. 'We don't need a court. There's me and John Weiss.' He indicated the storekeeper. 'That should be legal enough—two members of the city council.'

'I got a third one here.' Pete Quilter came up out of the snowy darkness. He had Ira Forrester by the collar, a frightened and chastened man. 'He admits he knew what was going to happen tonight.'

'Nothing about a killing!' the livery owner protested feebly. 'I'm against killing! I told Lenson—'

Rigby the newspaperman said, 'I'd guess that about settles it!'

Stormont looked over the group, reading their temper. He shrugged. 'All right. Bring him along, if that's your mood; let's have it out. I hope at least some of you have brought guns!'

There was no shouting, almost no sound as they made their march up the long street; the snow, that was beginning by now to gather in the hard ruts, muffled their boots. After the excitement of dynamiting and gunplay at the freight office, the town had turned abnormally quiet. The steadily tramping group of men took a wide corner and then the high, lamp-splashed bulk of Lenson's reared ahead.

Stormont ordered two of his men to cover the rear of the building. With the others behind him, he went up the broad steps and flung open the frosted-glass doors. The jangle of the battered piano burst out on the night. Then this, and every other sound, abruptly quit.

Stormont spotted three men he knew to be followers of Lat Roan. In silence he pointed them out; he told the rest, 'We're in no mood to fool with you. But anyone that don't want trouble, won't have any with us.'

Pete Quilter saw a houseman reaching for a

hideout gun under his faro table and stopped him with a warning. 'Watch those bartenders,' Stormont ordered. Then, crossing the big room, he moved directly to the door marked PRIVATE. He expected to find it locked but the knob gave under his hand and he pushed it open, only to find Murray Lenson's office dark and deserted. He frowned and turned back to the bar.

'Where is he?'

The two bartenders exchanged an uneasy look. One shrugged elaborately. 'He never said.'

'A night like this,' Stormont said, 'I doubt he'd ride far.'

John Weiss suggested, 'He's got him a room upstairs, hasn't he?'

Stormont glanced at the steps leading up to a gallery, and a hallway lined with doors. 'Is that right?' he demanded.

The bartender admitted it reluctantly. 'The one at the rear.'

Stormont shared a look and a nod with Pete Quilter. To the rest of his men he said, 'Hold them quiet.' Then he and Quilter turned to the stairs.

The hall leading back from the balcony was a short one, only three doors on each side that opened on private card rooms. The wall lamps in their brass fixtures were unlighted, the doors stood open on dark interiors. But beneath the final door on the left, a pencil line of yellow light showed. Quilter nudged his companion. 'I see it,' Stormont said. At the end of the hall were more stairs leading below. 'Keep an eye on those,' he added shortly.

'Ain't I going in with you?'

'If Lenson's in there, I want a few words with him. Maybe I can soften him up.'

Quilter scrutinized him closely, then shrugged. 'I guess you know what you're doing . . .' He moved back toward the dark stairwell, to wait with a gun in hand.

Stormont lifted his hand to knock, then instead dropped it to the china knob. As he hesitated, he thought he heard movement within the room, decided he had been mistaken. He checked Pete Quilter's position with a glance; deliberately, he twisted the knob and threw the door swiftly open.

Murray Lenson lay fully dressed on the bed, a copy of an Oklahoma City newspaper open in his hands. He let the paper settle across his chest as he stared at the intruder, during a long count that gave Stormont time to tally the room hastily.

As a living quarters it was crude enough—barely large enough for the white-painted bed and a couple of straight chairs. Though Stormont looked for a gun, he didn't see one.

As he heeled the door shut behind him, the other man found his tongue. 'Didn't you ever hear that doors were to knock on?'

'I was in a hurry.' Stormont showed him the

gun in his hand. 'Now, get up from there and put on your shoes. You're going with me.'

The man looked at the gun but made no move to obey. 'Maybe you'll tell me what this is all about!'

'Your friend Lat Roan is dead. That give you a clue, maybe?'

He saw Lenson's head jerk as the news hit him. But the movement threw his eyes into shadow and his frowning face revealed nothing. 'Why should it?' he demanded flatly. And then, after the slightest of hesitations, 'What happened?'

'As if you didn't know, he tried to take the safe at Chapman's. A man in the office—Paul Lavery—was killed. That makes it murder! And we've got a witness that you were the one planned the thing.'

Murray Lenson let a sneer lift his full upper lip. 'What witness?'

'Forrester.'

The sneer faded. This news plainly had its effect. For that one moment, Lenson's confidence was really shaken. And Stormont moved the barrel of the gun a little as he said crisply, 'I'm waiting, mister!'

The saloon owner tossed the newspaper away, to skim across the bed and float to the floor on the other side of it. He lifted his stockinged feet off the bed and swung to a sitting position; he leaned his weight on his fists as he peered, scowling, up at Stormont.

He said suddenly, 'Let's not move too fast! What if I was to tell you—your friend Ivy was involved in the job, too? That make any difference?'

'None at all. I already knew it—and anyway, he's dead. You can't buy me off with that!'

The man's eyes narrowed. The planes of his face reflected the lamplight greasily; he was sweating, though the room itself—heated by a grating that let warmth rise from the lower story of the saloon—wasn't particularly warm.

He said, 'There's Paul Lavery . . .'

Unnamed, half-recognized suspicions clutched at Stormont. His hand squeezed the gun butt until hurt knuckles protested. 'What about Lavery?'

'Why, who did you think told us Chapman would be out of the office at traintime tonight? Who'd you think arranged to let Roan and Ivy in, by unfastening the gate?' The man's lips curled, as he saw Stormont's reaction. 'Hell, Stormont! He told me himself you were sweet on his wife! How do you think she's going to like having his name smeared all over this mess—and hers too? You take me in, and I swear I'll do a job on all three of you!'

The hand holding the gun began to tremble. 'You can't do anything to hurt me, or Lavery either,' he retorted. 'But, by God, you cause that woman grief and I'll kill you! I could do it right now!' The mocking look faded from the sweat-shining face, was replaced by a first hint of fear. Lenson must have known he'd made a mistake this time. He remained silent, watching Stormont.

The latter straightened his shoulders, pulled in a long breath that was tanged by the scent of the cigar smoldering on the table edge. 'There *is* one deal I'd be willing to make you,' he said crisply. 'And only one! Tom Chapman's not going to be too concerned about a robbery that didn't come off. What he wants is the man who sent raiders against his freight wagons. I know who that man was, but I can't prove it.'

He paused, giving Lenson a chance to pick up his cue; but the other only looked at him. His mouth tightened. 'You got no love for Hayes McClure. Give us a case against him and I think Tom will be satisfied to let you off with just getting out of town. Otherwise we're going to hold you for Bill Tilghman and a federal court.

'Well, what's your answer?' he prodded, and then broke off seeing the remarkable change in Murray Lenson's broad face. All at once the man was shaking, his mouth open on words that wouldn't come, his eyes pinned on Stormont. Frowning, trying to fathom what could have put the man in such terror, Stormont stared back. And then his eye was drawn to the table at Lenson's elbow, as the long-forming ash on the cigar resting there broke of its own weight and dropped silently to the floor.

Suddenly the tang of the burning tobacco was sharp and insistent in his nostrils, and a silent voice was shouting its warning: *When did Murray Lenson start smoking cigars?* He knew the answer then and it pulled him around, toward the closet, even as the curtain rings sang along the rod. The cloth was torn aside, he saw the man hidden there and the faint shine of a gun barrel. Before it could fire, he whipped his own weapon up and worked the trigger.

The bucking of the gun wrenched his hurt hand but this time he kept hold of it. Concussion smote his eardrums, filled his head. Through the burst of muzzle smoke he saw Hayes McClure sag forward and catch himself against the frame of the opening. McClure's gun dropped at his feet, unfired, and his carefully shaven face was white with the pain of the wrist he clutched against him.

Boots pounded in the hall; Pete Quilter slammed the door wide. He halted on the threshold, staring—ready with the help he suddenly saw wasn't needed.

And through the ringing in his head, Stormont was aware of Murray Lenson crying anxiously, 'Listen, Stormont. Do you hear me? I said, I'll take that deal!'

* * *

Gib Yaeger said, 'By thunder, this is great

news! She's gonna be a new town, now you're rid of Lenson and that saloon. And sounds like your boss might be over the worst of *his* trouble, too.'

'But it's such a shame,' his wife said, 'about Paul Lavery! Whatever can you tell his wife?'

Yaeger nodded, frowning as he thought of this. He sat with awl and leather and baling wire in front of him, trying to mend an ancient bit of harness. The work had lain forgotten as he listened to the account of last night's happenings. 'Maybe you'd like us to tell her?' he suggested.

Stormont shook his head. 'No. I think she should hear it from me. It's why I rode out here this morning.'

'That's up to you. She's over on the other claim. Don't know what she finds to do over there. She can never hope to prove it up, now—by herself. Not that her husband was an awful lot of help.'

'You want to make any bets?' Stormont said, and got up from the trestle table that filled most of the room. 'This isn't going to stop Jean Lavery! I don't think anything could . . .'

Yaeger nodded. 'You could be right.'

Stormont picked up his hat, and looked around. An air of peace lay upon the sod house. The baby slept in its packing-case crib; a stew simmered over the fire; beyond the window, morning sunlight flooded the red land from a sky left cloudless, after the wind and brief snowstorm of yesterday. He was astonished at the sense of permanence he found here. You could almost feel that here, indeed, was a place where a man and his woman could make a home, and have children, and pass the future on to them. For Stormont, it was an odd experience.

Martha Yaeger said, 'I'm so sorry about your friend.'

'Bill Ivy?' He shrugged. 'He chose his own way of going. It was his life, and he was a restless man.'

'How about you, Stormont?' Gib Yaeger asked, looking at him closely. 'With this business cleared up, Chapman's affairs ought to be dropping into shape pretty quick. I imagine you'll be able to move on.'

Stormont hesitated. He was aware of the crumpled piece of paper in his pocket, the registration on the Pecan Creek claim. How could he explain to these people what he hardly understood himself? He'd seen men as little alike as Bill Ivy and Paul Lavery moving restlessly, rootlessly through life, hunting something they couldn't name. He knew how the search had ended for both of them—in total waste. The ending could be the same for himself.

Unless their example had taught him what those two had never learned . . .

Rather than try to explain this, he shrugged

and said merely, 'I always did like this country. And Chapman's not getting younger, so there's going to be plenty to do. Guess I'll stay around.' He added, 'Besides, there's a quarter section I thought I might try proving up on.'

Gib Yaeger stared. 'This don't sound like the Stormont we met two months ago!' And then a new thought made him grin. 'Could it be Miss Lucy Chapman has something to do with changing your mind?'

'Lucy?' It was Stormont's turn to stare. 'What gives everybody that notion? Oh, at one time, maybe; but—we had a long talk this morning. We'll always be the best of friends, but I'm too old for her!'

'You ain't all *that* much too old!'

Martha Yaeger had been watching Stormont with a look of understanding; he had an odd feeling that she knew much about him a mere man could fail to see. Now she silenced her husband, saying almost sharply, 'Be quiet, Gibson! You don't know what you're talking about!'

Martha Yaeger came to Stormont and laid a hand on his arm. 'And never fear about Jean. What you have to tell her will be hard; but there's nothing time can't fix. Just let it.'

He smiled, and nodded, and went out into the November morning. The deep sky rang like a bell, the crisp bracing air of morning filled a man's lungs with a heady raciness. As Stormont rose to the saddle and turned his roan in the direction of the Lavery claim, Jody Yaeger came racing up across the fields calling, 'Wait for me, Mr. Stormont! I want to go with you.'

'Jody!' his mother called sharply. And his father added, 'You remain here, boy.'

Jody knew when his parents meant business. Grinning, not at all resentful, he hauled up and lifted a hand to wave Stormont on. Stormont returned the salute, and touched his horse with the spurs.

Some rags of yesterday's first snowfall lay caught in the hollows of the frozen red earth, and in the furrows of Gib Yaeger's plowing. Trees stood bare above the half-finished shell of the sod house on the Lavery claim. As he rode up, he saw Jean Lavery standing with a shawl about her hair, and full skirts streaming in the ground wind. Her arm was raised to shade her eyes as she watched him come.

Lee Stormont knew she recognized him. From the way she stood—so quietly waiting—he had a strange feeling she already knew what it was he'd come to tell her . . .